## Garek has a troubled soul.

Garek watched the shadows dance across Brianna's face in the light of the flickering torch.

He yearned for something he could not put a name to.

Reaching out, he lifted a lock of her curly brown hair, stroking it between his fingers. She watched him, her eyes wide.

"There is more, Garek, is there not? Something you have kept from me?"

Surprised at her use of his given name, he stilled. He abruptly dropped her hair from his fingers. "Why do you ask such a thing?"

She said nothing, waiting for him to continue. He returned to his seat, throwing himself upon the stool that creaked alarmingly under his weight. Brianna followed him, seating herself again on her stool. Minutes went by and still he said nothing.

Brianna was growing weary, realizing that several hours had passed since she had entered the keep. As tired as she was, she remained stoically seated upon the stool, waiting for him to speak.

When he turned to her, there was anguish in his eyes.

"I killed my wife."

**DARLENE MINDRUP** is a full-time homemaker and homeschool teacher. A "radical feminist" turned "radical Christian," Darlene lives in Arizona with her husband and two children. She believes "romance is for everyone, not just the young and beautiful."

**Other books by Darlene Mindrup**

HEARTSONG PRESENTS
HP207—The Eagle and the Lamb
HP224—Edge of Destiny
HP243—The Rising Son

Don't miss out on any of our super romances. Write to us at the following address for information on our newest releases and club information.

Heartsong Presents Readers' Service
PO Box 719
Uhrichsville, OH 44683

# A Light Within

*Darlene Mindrup*

*Heartsong Presents*

I would like to thank Rosie and LeRoy Mindrup for sharing their son with me. I know he's the man he is because of the parents you were.

And I wish to thank Rebecca Germany for having the patience to put up with a fledgling author. Every author should have an editor like Rebecca!

**A note from the author:**
*I love to hear from my readers! You may correspond with me by writing:* **Darlene Mindrup**
**Author Relations**
**PO Box 719**
**Uhrichsville, OH 44683**

**ISBN 1-57748-335-9**

**A LIGHT WITHIN**

*Cover illustration by Chris Cocozza.*

PRINTED IN THE U.S.A.

# prologue

At the beginning of its history, the land now known as England was shrouded in mystery. Little is known of the first human inhabitants, but they are believed to have been Stone Age cave dwellers.

Between 8000 and 3000 B.C., settlers arrived from as far away as Spain and Brittany, in northern France. These people settled among the hilltops of southern England.

Other people migrated there from the Rhine and Danube River regions of Europe. They wove cloth, mined tin, and made bronze tools. Among their most cryptic achievements were giant monoliths, such as those found at Stonehenge, that were believed to have been used as tribal gathering places and for astronomical inquiry.

The first invaders of England were the Celts, who brought their nature gods with them. Their priests, the Druids, with their secret rituals and dark magic, added to the mystery surrounding the isle.

When the Romans entered the small country, many of the secret practices of the Druids disappeared. The great Rome, although already set upon a path of self-destruction, brought peace and plenty to England—or Britannia as it was known at the time.

Finally, Roman soldiers were withdrawn from Britannia in order to protect their homeland's borders from warring invaders. With their departure, the small isle became helpless against the barbaric raiders who found the island among their sea travel routes.

With each invasion a portion of England developed its own history, until at last the Angles, Saxons, and Jutes established a kingdom known as Angle-land.

Torn apart by war, England fell into dark times. Superstition abounded, aided by the Christian church, which had been established during the Roman period. It was thought that only the clergy had the right to read God's Word, and that the people should listen to what the church instructed.

Education for the common man, and even for the noble, was practically nonexistent. Where there is lack of education, ignorance abounds.

The people eked out an existence while in subservience to whichever invading power proved stronger than the rest. They did not even hope for a different way of life, for no other way of life was known.

But into this darkness cut a ray of light. Though the people of England, finally united under one king, did not realize it, their final conqueror would set them free from the darkness that surrounded them.

Duke William of Normandy fell upon the land with a rigor the likes of which the small isle had never seen. A fierce warrior hated by many, William's rise to power as king of England brought much change to the land. With him, England began to prosper once again.

Among William's achievements were castles—first of wood, later of stone—that would finally secure the land from further invasions.

Since William was French, he also brought a new language to the country. Most of the English people continued to speak Old English, but those who wanted power learned French.

In time, conversing in French became fashionable, and many French words were taken by the English and added to their own language to form a new language, Middle English. After serving as king for over thirty years, this new language served finally to unite conqueror and conquered into one people.

## one

A cold mist lay over the English countryside, a precursor of the winter to come. A lone rider approached the small village in the gathering twilight, a large man riding an even larger horse. His clothing proclaimed him a knight, but the likes of which no one in this little hamlet had ever seen.

The black of his mail-link armor and his billowing cloak made the rider seem a colossus. A hawk rested quietly upon the arm he held out to his side, its feathers ruffled against the circling mist.

The dismal day well suited Garek du Mor's mood. Wherever he traveled across the English countryside, the Norman knight was met with hatred and fear. Although this bothered him little, the lives he had taken in response had made him bitter.

He stopped at the first hut he came to and called out. Receiving no reply, he grew aggravated, for evidence of occupation was obvious: smoke curled lazily through a small hole in the thatched roof, and a soft light peeked from the small apertures serving as windows in the daub and wattle walls.

Finally, a man stepped reluctantly out the front door. He was neither young nor old; Garek estimated him to be about a score plus ten.

The villein studied the knight silently, hatred and fear blazing from his amber eyes.

Doffing his helm, Garek fixed the man with a cold gray look that mirrored the leaden sky above. Shifting his mantle to the side, he exposed his huge broadsword.

"Be you free man or serf?" the deep voice rumbled from the depths of the big knight's chest. Although his French accent was obvious, his English was clear and articulate.

The man's chin lifted a notch. "Is any man free from the Normans?" he asked, bitterness evident in his voice.

Again Garek studied the man. "Perhaps not."

They continued to measure each another, one full of anger and bitterness, the other curious and suspicious.

Garek was about to speak again when the front door opened and a woman stepped out, her face hidden by the shawl thrown across her shoulders and around her face. Her trim shape was emphasized by the tightly cinched belt buckled at her waist. Garek wondered if her thin form was due to hunger.

As the knight's gaze wandered over the girl, the villein noticed the look and snapped at her angrily. The girl jerked to a stop, her eyes widening in alarm as she noticed for the first time the huge black-armored knight.

Her shawl slipped from her head to nestle against her shoulders, and for a moment Garek found himself staring into huge blue eyes before the maid hastily returned to the cottage.

Garek stared at the closed door and felt a strange urge to follow the girl. What had he seen in those incredible eyes that would give him such a thought?

"What is it you wish of me, milord?"

The villein's sharp voice brought Garek's thoughts quickly back to the mission at hand. His cold gaze settled on the man before him once again.

"How far to Castle Fenlac?"

Surprised, the villein took a quick step back. The fear seemed to intensify in his eyes; Garek could almost smell it emanating from his pores.

The man pointed down the road. "About an hour's ride that way. There is a shortcut through the woods, if you care to take it." His voice lowered and Garek was quick to pick out the menace behind the words. "But have a care, for the forests contain many dangers of their own."

Sensing the threat behind the words, Garek sharpened his

gaze on the man standing before him. He pushed his coif from his head, letting it rest across his shoulders, revealing the tousled blond locks beneath.

The villein's lips curled with contempt as he considered the Norman warrior with his short locks and clean face. His own full beard was his pride, and his brown hair lay long against his shoulders.

"What is your name?" Garek demanded; he saw the man's shoulders tense at the arrogance of the tone.

"Edward," he returned grudgingly.

The hawk on Garek's arm spread his wings and screeched a warning as another man appeared from around the side of the hut. Before Garek could respond, the man turned and disappeared from sight.

One blond eyebrow rose, but the villein offered nothing and Garek decided not to ask. There was something amiss here, but Garek didn't have time to find out what it was. Already the twilight was deepening.

Without another word, Garek turned his snorting destrier back to the road, not once looking back—though he was certain that if he had, the man would still be there. Garek could feel the man's eyes upon his back.

The mist seemed to be thickening into rain as Garek found the shortcut through the woods. His horse shied nervously as he prodded it forward, dark, shadowy fingers thickening all around them. "Easy, Corbeau," Garek soothed, patting the beast's huge neck, though he was none too relaxed himself.

He was not a fearful man, but having the trees close in around him gave him pause. It wasn't the things of the forest or the night that he feared, but the two-legged English miscreants who refused to accept William as their rightful king and even now were trying to gather their scattered people together to form a rebellion.

The previous lord of this manor had been killed under suspicious circumstances—in a riding accident, as he was surveying his holdings in response to King William's request.

William had been furious and would have leveled the whole countryside in his wrath, but he chose instead to send Garek to seek answers and to maintain this essential holding until the English could be made to see reason. Garek had no intention of succumbing to the same fate as his predecessor.

He hadn't gone far when a movement to his left caught his eye. Reining his horse to a stop, he studied the darkening forest carefully, his soldier's instincts on full alert.

In the darkening twilight, he could scarcely make out a figure moving quickly toward him through the trees. He could see only one, but there could be others hiding in the dense foliage all around him.

His heart began to race as the adrenaline pumped through his veins, and in one swift movement he sent his hawk screeching into the air as he drew his sword from its scabbard, ready for battle.

&

Brianna leaned her back against the wooden door, breathing rapidly. Her shawl dropped heedlessly to the floor as she moved to the small window opening at the front of the hut. The shutters had been left ajar so that some of the smoke from the fire pit in the middle of the room could escape.

She could hear the voices of the big Norman and her brother, but she could not make out what was being said. Her breath caught in her throat as she watched the man sitting so casually on his mount. Never had she seen such a large, imposing man.

What was the Norman knight doing here? And all alone? She thought of the previous knight that had been given this fief by King William. That knight had been nothing like this dark warrior.

Closing her eyes, she again pictured the man's cold gray eyes as they had bored into hers. The darkness of his clothing seemed to well match his soul, yet in the moment their eyes had met, Brianna had seemed to see pain that was quickly veiled. Something within her had responded to the pain she beheld there.

Her brother would be less than pleased with her thoughts, for he hated the Normans with a passion. He would never accept William as king, but why would it matter to her which man claimed to rule this earthly sod? Brianna longed for the day when the true ruler of all the earth would return, taking her home to be with Him. She was tired unto death of all the killing and hatred.

The screech of the hawk returned her attention to what was going on outside. From the corner of her eye she noticed Thomas, the tanner. He was there for only a moment, then gone. Brianna felt herself go cold, for Thomas's presence could only mean one thing.

Another moment and her brother came into the house. He noticed Brianna at the window and frowned. "Get away from there."

She quickly did as she was told. Edward had a nasty temper and she had already tested it that day. The huge purpling bruise on her cheek gave mute testimony to the fact.

A knock sounded at the door and Edward quickly opened it, motioning the figure inside. Thomas entered, his eyes swiftly going from Edward to Brianna and back again.

"He is headed for the castle. Get the others," Edward told him. Without a word Thomas slipped quietly back out the door.

"What are you going to do?" Brianna asked her brother fearfully.

He barely glanced her way as he went to the table in the corner to retrieve his knife. Shoving it down inside the belt of his tunic, he turned to Brianna. "Never mind. I will return shortly."

"Edward!"

"Be quiet!" Glaring at her, he flung open the door and left.

Brianna paced the confining space of their small hut, twisting her hands in agony. She had been unable to help the previous lord, but could she do something to help this man, whoever he was? She couldn't let him be murdered when it was within her power to stop it.

Lips set with resolve, Brianna grabbed her woolen mantle from the peg behind the door and hurried out into the fast-approaching night.

ॐ

A small figure detached itself from the forest to his left and made its way in wraithlike silence to Garek's side. A shiver flashed through him as a slim white hand reached up and pushed the mantle hood back, revealing the young maid he had seen at the villein's cottage. Huge doelike eyes regarded him in silent entreaty, but he had no idea what she desired.

"Milord, a moment please." The melodious tone of her voice had a soothing effect on the knight and he slowly sheathed his sword. Lifting his arm, he made a loud screeching sound. A moment later his call was returned in kind, and Brianna could see a hawk circling overhead. Fascinated, she watched as the hawk glided downward, its wings back and claws extended. It landed with a soft thud against the knight's gauntlet.

Turning back to the girl, Garek tried to see her through the dim light. Her features were not clear, but the bruise on the side of her cheek was unmistakable.

His eyes again met hers, and Brianna read momentary sympathy there before his face took on a closed appearance.

"Speak," he told her, his voice cold.

Hesitantly, she approached his huge war horse, at the same time keeping a wary eye on the hawk. How old could she be, Garek wondered. She looked no older than a child. He could see her hands tremble at her sides as she moved closer. Something stirred in him that he hadn't felt for a very long time, and he didn't relish the feeling now.

Frowning, he tried to shake off the compassion he felt for the maid. Such sentiment only weakened a man, made him vulnerable; but for some unknown reason, he wanted to know more about this girl.

Licking suddenly dry lips, Brianna raised her gaze to Garek's face. He was a handsome man, though a scar ran from one side of his forehead to just above his right cheekbone. Fleetingly, Brianna wondered how he had come by it, for it was obviously not a recent wound.

"Milord, I beg you reconsider going farther into the woods."

Instantly alert, Garek's eyes narrowed coldly on her face. "What say you?"

Biting her bottom lip, Brianna tried again. "There are things in these woods that are dangerous. It is not wise to travel them alone at night. Especially not this night."

The warning was unmistakable, and Garek wondered why the maid should choose to caution an enemy. He looked forward along the road as though trying to see what lay ahead. Turning his attention once more to the girl, he settled back against his saddle.

"What is your name?"

"Brianna, milord."

Garek dismounted and Brianna hastily stepped out of his way as he settled the hawk on the pommel of his saddle. She had to look a long way up to see his features, straining to see them in the near darkness.

Seemingly of its own volition, Garek's hand raised and gently stroked the swollen bruise on the girl's cheek. His voice was soft when he spoke.

"Why seek you to save me, wench?"

Heart thudding in response to his gentle touch, Brianna could only stare at him. Why had she sought to warn him? Edward would consider her a traitor to England, and perhaps she was, but she'd had enough of death and vengeance to last her a lifetime.

But then again, that was not it either. There was something about this giant of a man that had softened her heart. What was it about him that could do this?

Garek's eyes hardened perceptibly. "Or perhaps you fear for some other? Tell me plainly what you know."

"Milord, I cannot."

Growing angry, Garek grasped her by her upper arms, his fingers biting into her flesh. "Someone waits in the wood? Is this what you are trying to say?" When she didn't answer, he shook her slightly. "Is it?"

She could only nod her head, biting her lip in agitation. Releasing her, he glared down the road before looking back to Brianna. "How many?"

Brianna shrugged her shoulders and then realized he probably could not see the movement in the now complete darkness. "I know not," she told him, and he could hear the sincerity in her voice.

Garek stood motionless a long time, trying to decide his best course of action. He didn't altogether believe the maid though something about her inspired his trust. Sighing, he turned to Brianna. "Return to your home. I am in your debt."

"What will you do?" she asked him.

He didn't answer. Turning, he took his hawk upon his arm and swiftly mounted his horse. Surprised at her willingness to do so, Brianna reached out and gripped the reins he held clasped in his hand. "Please, milord. You won't kill them?"

It was then that Garek realized the woman's husband must be involved. His gray eyes turned to slate. Had the woman betrayed her own husband and then hoped for Garek's mercy, or did she perhaps hope that he would slay the man and so free her from his obviously abusive company? He almost snarled at the thought. All women were an unfaithful lot and no one knew it better than he!

Jerking the reins from her hands, Garek spurred his destrier into a gallop. He could hear the woman calling to him from behind, but he closed his ears to the sound. Dark demons from his past reared their ugly heads and his anger grew. He welcomed the challenge of a good fight. That he was alone did not bother him. He was beyond reason.

❧

Edward motioned to Thomas on his left, alerting him to the approaching steed. There were only six of them, but with surprise on their side, William would soon be minus one more knight. Thomas could see the gleam of Edward's teeth as he grinned to himself in the dark.

As the huge horse drew abreast of them, Edward whistled sharply and all six men moved as one, quickly surrounding the horse.

The destrier rared in fright, his mammoth hooves pawing the air around him. One of Edward's compatriots received a blow from the flaying hooves that sent him senseless to the dirt of the road.

Jerking away from the men, the riderless horse ran several steps forward before stopping. Shaking his flowing mane, he neighed nervously at the five surprised men staring after him.

"Looking for someone?"

Whirling in the direction of the soft voice, Edward's eyes grew large as he saw the figure standing behind them on the road. The huge Norman seemed one with the night, his black mantle flowing around him in the darkness. The hissing intakes of breath told Edward of his friends' reaction to the sight.

Even in the darkness, the gleam of the warrior's sword was unmistakable. Knowing that knives and pitchforks would have no effect against the dark lord's mail, the others fled into the forest, leaving Edward to face his enemy alone.

They stood thus, face to face, though neither could see the other's visage clearly in the darkness.

"Come on, you Saxon swine!" Garek roared. "Or are you too much a coward without your friends beside you?"

Edward considered attacking the man where he stood, so great was his hatred, but even the red haze of his anger did not cloud his reason enough that he would risk his own life. After all, when all was said and done, he was the coward Garek accused him of being.

Picking up a rock from beside the road, Edward threw it at the Norman, and in the second it took for Garek to avoid the missile, Edward had disappeared into the forest.

Although it had been too dark to see any of his attackers' faces, Garek was certain one of them was the villein from the village—the blue-eyed woman's husband.

Knowing the foolishness of trying to track his attackers among the trees in the dark, Garek mounted his horse and, turning, retraced his steps until he found the tree he looked for. Lifting his gloved hand to the lowest branch, he retrieved his hawk.

"So, Lebeau," he told the animal. "These English are a cowardly lot, are they not?"

The hawk cocked its head, its normally rapier-sharp vision impeded by the hood covering its head. Laughing without humor, Garek made his way down the road toward the castle. What might be waiting for him there, he knew not.

Soon Garek left the forest. The road continued ahead of him, and in the distance he could see the towering motte rising darkly against the moonlit sky.

There was no watchman on the gate tower to announce him, but Garek hadn't expected one. Chevier, the previous lord here, had brought his own men with him from France, and upon his death they had returned to the continent.

There seemed to be no other living creature about, and the hawk gave no sign of anyone's presence. Even Corbeau remained calm, his strides eating up the miles to the drawbridge over the moat surrounding the outer bailey.

Garek crossed the wooden bridge that allowed him entrance into the middle bailey area that surrounded the palisade walls of the castle. He stopped midway, staring down at the murky depths of the water fed by a river he could just discern meandering behind the castle.

Very few of the castles King William and his brother Odo had built thus far could boast a wet moat. Chevier had chosen his castle site well.

Urging his steed onward, Garek passed through the gates and into the inner bailey, the courtyard. All he could see in the darkness were dim shapes of buildings, the castle tower rising majestically before him.

The size of the building surprised Garek. It stood at least three levels high. How had Chevier managed to raise such a fortification as Fenlac in such a short time? Perhaps the complaints of the English people had been justified after all.

Odo, Garek knew, had forced the inhabitants of the island to build fortifications all over England, regardless of their need to tend their crops. That, he was sure, was only one reason the people stared at Garek in open hostility.

Returning to the gate, Garek dropped the portcullis, closing off the outside world. He gazed through the lattice bars, searching the forest in the distance for any sign of life. Having no desire to be closed in a building for the night, especially one that might harbor hidden enemies, he made camp near the outside well.

Garek found two large sticks and tied them together with a leather thong, making a cross. Pounding it into the ground, he then settled his hawk on the perch.

He spoke to Corbeau as he brushed him down by the light of the fire. One thing remained uppermost in his mind.

"Why would a woman marry such a man as that?" he asked his faithful steed. He shook his head. "It is beyond reason. Aye, all women are beyond reason. Be glad you don't have to deal with them, my friend."

His thoughts returned to the confrontation on the road. He had left one man lying there, believing his companions would retrieve him and tend to his wounds. As for Garek, he had neither the time nor the inclination.

Such cold hatred he had seen in Edward's eyes. He could sense there was more to the man's hate than anger at having been conquered by a foreign king.

There were others in this country with much the same sentiment. He had seen it before and doubtless would again. Wouldn't he feel much the same?

His lip curled up in a sneer. Every Englishman he had encountered thus far had wanted his blood. Save one, that is.

His features softened as the white face of the village maid who had met him on the road floated into his mind. For a brief moment his thoughts relaxed, as did his features. But only for a moment.

# two

The morning sun was just beginning to rise when Garek made his way across the bailey and stood at the foot of the castle steps. He stared upward at the mammoth log structure. Fifteen stone steps led to the front portal that opened onto the main floor of the building.

The ground-level floor was used for storage of food stuffs and smaller animals. Garek opened the lower door and carefully peered inside before entering the dark chamber. He walked from one side of the building to the other, his eyes adjusting to the dim light that filtered in from the small window openings around the perimeter of the room.

There were no animals or supplies anywhere. It was evident the villeins of the area had made use of any provisions that had been left by Chevier's men. Only the fetid smell of decaying hay and animal excrement gave evidence that there had ever been any occupants to the building.

Wrinkling his nose with distaste, Garek hurried from the cellar and mounted the outside stairs to the floor above. He slammed the huge door inward, following swiftly, his broadsword drawn and ready.

This, then, was the main hall, he decided, since a huge fire pit stood in the middle of the room. A dais at one end held a table that Garek assumed was where Chevier and his guests had eaten. It was not a simple trestle table but one hewn of fine solid oak; Garek believed Chevier had used it to impress others with his status.

The room held an assortment of benches and mats that would have been used by the castle servants and knights for sleeping. Why hadn't the villeins taken these articles along with the others? Shrugging, Garek turned to a door at his right that separated one end of the huge hall from the main room.

Again being careful, Garek slowly opened the door and peered inside. The remains of another fire pit rested at one end of the room, the stone floor around it charred and blackened.

The only other furnishings were a huge table and a broken bench.

Garek would have turned and left the room, but a slight movement behind the table caught his eye. Readying himself for attack, he called out in English, "Come out. I know you are there."

A moment later a frightened face peered around the end of the table—a boy no more than ten plus four years of age, Garek surmised.

"Come out, boy," Garek told him, sheathing his sword. "I will not harm you."

The boy sidled out from behind the table, his eyes huge in a gaunt face. He quietly regarded Garek, twining his fingers in front of him in agitation.

"What is your name, boy, and why are you here?"

"Gaylan, milord. I. . .I live here."

Garek's eyebrows flew upward, but he awaited an explanation.

"I. . .I served Lord Chevier," he told Garek hesitantly. "I helped Mary in the kitchen."

"And where is this Mary?" Garek asked, his eyes roaming the empty chamber.

"She left with the others after. . .after Lord Chevier's death. They were afraid of what his knights might do."

Garek studied the boy thoughtfully. His hair was long, in the Saxon style, but his face was clean shaven. Was that because the lad had yet to grow hair upon his face? He certainly seemed young.

"And why are you still here?"

The boy dropped his eyes. "I have nowhere else to go." He lifted worried eyes to Garek's face. "Are you the new Lord of Fenlac?"

"Aye," Garek affirmed. "And I have need of servants for the hall. My men will be here sometime today with supplies, but I will need an accounting of this holding." Garek turned his cold gray gaze upon the young man. "You know of this shire?"

Bobbing his head, the boy told him, "Aye, milord. I know most everyone around here, though there is a girl in the village who probably knows more."

"Who is this girl? Can you bring her to me?"

"Her name is Brianna. She lives just at the end of the village."

Garek jerked his attention back to the boy. "I have met her." Garek's thoughts turned to that meeting on the road. So, the wench knew most of the people in the shire. A slow smile spread across his face. "Yes, bring her to me. And any others who might be willing to serve in this hall. Go quickly, and be back before nightfall."

Walking with the boy down to the drawbridge, Garek lifted the portcullis and allowed the boy to pass before securing the chains to leave the gate raised.

He went back to his horse, pulling grain from his own bags and putting it into the feed bag he hung over the horse's head.

Turning to the hawk, he lifted his arm and the bird leapt onto his forearm, its wings fluttering as it tried to gain its balance.

"Time to break our fast, huh, Lebeau?" Garek stroked the bird's feathers softly before lifting him into the air. "Chassez!" he commanded, then watched as the bird circled high into the sky searching for food.

Several hours later, Garek sat back against the stone wall of the well, sighing as he threw the last of the bones of a small rabbit onto the fire beside him.

"You have done well, Lebeau," he told the bird and threw it another chunk of raw meat. Garek leaned back and studied the sky overhead. The sun shone weakly through the morning mist, trying to burn it away.

Garek shook his head in irritation. England and its infernal rains! Why would any man choose to live in this soggy place?

Scrambling to his feet, Garek decided to check the palisade walls and the buildings that surrounded the main keep.

He was strolling along the bulwark inspecting the strength and security of the log walls when he noticed the contingent of knights making their way toward the bridge.

Without realizing it, he felt himself relax for the first time in days.

"Ho, Etienne," he called down, returning the grin of the younger knight below.

"Ho, Garek! All is well with you?"

"Aye." Garek's grin broadened. "You doubted it?"

Sir Etienne Bolson shrugged his shoulders. "One never knows. These English are a treacherous lot."

Garek climbed down to meet his men as they entered the middle bailey. Their pages and squires brought up the rear, arguing good-naturedly among themselves as to the best location for the wagons and supplies.

Garek ended their bickering by showing them where to stow their stores.

Sir Bolson stood studying the castle fortification. He shook his head slowly in amazement. "How did Chevier manage to build all of this in less than a year?"

Garek's eyes followed his. "I have heard much complaining as I traveled across this land. It would seem that Odo and King William are bent on covering the land with castles, and they care not how they have to build them, as long as they are built."

Shrugging, Bolson turned to his companion. "It is understandable. Had England the castles to begin with, Harold would probably still be king instead of rotting in the ground. William would not have found it so easy to conquer a fortified land. He realizes this and is determined that the same thing will not happen to him."

"Aye," Garek agreed, "but the English are being abused, I am afraid, so that William has what he desires."

Bolson cocked an eyebrow at Garek. "You think Chevier did the same?"

"As you suggested, how could such a castle have been built in such a short time otherwise?"

Late in the afternoon, Garek decided to take Bolson and a few others and scout the surrounding countryside. He left most of his contingent behind, grunting at his orders to straighten some of the rooms in the keep and to clean out the stable. If not for their loyalty to Garek, he knew he would have a serious problem, for all were knights and not disposed to play the part of serf.

After leaving the castle behind, Garek exited the road to skirt the fields beyond the small copse of woods that bordered the property.

They hadn't traveled far when Garek noticed a small brown heap lying in the pathway before them. Curious, he moved his horse on an intercept course. As they drew near, a small moan drifted from the object, causing Garek's huge black to rear in surprise.

Garek fought with the beast, struggling to bring him back under control. "Easy, Corbeau! Down!"

The destrier quieted, a quiver of muscles rippling along his smooth back.

Bolson was already beside the bundle that Garek could now see was a human. Quickly dismounting, he joined the knight.

"By all that is holy!" Bolson hissed between his teeth, his horrified eyes lifting quickly to Garek's face.

Garek knelt beside the still form. Blood had congealed on

what he could see of the face. Turning the body over carefully, he came face to face with the young girl from the village. What was her name? Ah, yes. Brianna.

His breath drew in sharply at the sorry sight she presented. The bruise he saw last night was still dark and ugly against her cheek, but many others had been added since then. Her eyes were swollen shut, her lip cut and bleeding.

Garek gently pulled back the girl's mantle to check the extent of her injuries. Lash marks crisscrossed her arms and back, the blood already clotting against the welts. He felt for a pulse and was reassured to find it beating weakly against his fingers.

"Who could have done such a thing?"

Bolson's hoarse voice brought Garek's head snapping up. Lips tight, he gently lifted the girl into his arms. Striding to his horse, he set her gently against the pommel, climbing swiftly up behind her.

Triden, Barough, and Serin, the other knights who had accompanied him, stared in open-mouthed amazement. The girl had been beaten so badly, she hardly looked human at all.

Reining his horse around, Garek moved swiftly but as gently as he could. Brianna moaned in pain but remained unconscious.

Garek thundered into the courtyard, his horse's hooves tearing up the sod. Bellowing loudly, his men hastily exited the keep and stable, their swords drawn and ready.

Bolson took the girl from Garek's arms as he dismounted. Claiming her again when his feet hit the ground, Garek hastened inside.

Swiftly he climbed to the master's chambers he had found earlier that day. He lowered Brianna gently to the mattress, pushing the dusty furs aside as he did so.

"What will you do?" Bolson, who had followed him into the room, asked in concern.

"I do not know. I need a physician, but I have no idea

where to find one. The only one I know of who could help me is out seeing about servants for the hall."

"Do you think the girl will die?"

Garek's chin set in determination. "Not if I can help it. Take some of the knights. Search the village. If you find a physician, or someone who knows the healing arts, bring that one to me." His eyes grew darker. "And find me the villein named Edward. He lives on the outskirts of the village—the last house. Bring him also."

Bolson left and Garek began to gently remove Brianna's mantle. As the extent of her injuries became clear to him, he felt his anger begin to rise.

What had happened to the girl? Had she been attacked after he left her on the road? Had she lain there all night with no one to help? Guilt washed through him. He should have seen her safely home instead of charging off to do battle with a bunch of cowardly Saxons.

It seemed an eternity before the boy Gaylan returned. Garek could hear his voice from the courtyard below and realized that one of his knights must be telling him what had happened.

The boy entered the room, followed closely by a young woman. Garek's eyes momentarily rested on her, registering her dusky beauty. Her eyes met his boldly before Garek turned his attention to the boy once again.

"Is there a physician in this shire?"

"Yea, milord. His name is Alfred."

"Go quickly and bring him to me."

Gaylan's eyes went beyond Garek to the form lying on the bed. His breath hissed sharply. "Dear God!" Stepping backward, he hastily crossed himself. Without another word he rushed to do as bidden.

Garek turned his attention back to the woman who was watching him with open curiosity. He motioned toward Brianna, and although he had removed most of her clothing, he had left her torn kirtle.

"See to her," he commanded, and for the first time the woman noticed the figure on the bed. Her eyes went wide with shock as they flew back to Garek. He could read the message there.

"Nay, it was not my hand that wrought this."

Crossing to the bed, she studied the girl before sucking in a breath and falling on her knees beside her.

"Brianna!"

"You know her?"

The woman was already using the rag Garek had left in the bowl of water and was gently wiping blood from Brianna's face. "Yea, milord. Everyone knows Brianna."

Growing more curious, Garek's eyes studied the beaten figure. "Have you any idea who would do such a thing to her?"

"I have my ideas," she almost snarled in return.

Garek hesitated a moment before asking gently, "Was it her husband?"

The woman turned, surprised. "She has no husband."

Brows knitting in confusion, Garek's eyes went from one to the other. "A tall man with dark brown hair and eyes?"

The woman was shaking her head. "Nay, not her husband— her brother. And he has beaten her before, but never like this." Garek watched the woman as she cared for the girl, making soft cooing sounds of encouragement. Realizing there was nothing more he could do, he turned to the door.

"Call me if she wakes. I will send the physician to you when they return." He stopped at the threshold. "What is your name?"

"Mary, milord," she answered absently without turning around. She seemed to have forgotten her earlier fear of him.

A fetching woman, Garek decided. Sultry. Her dark beauty and green eyes would tempt any man. Save one.

Garek turned away. Beauty held no allure for him anymore, for he'd already had a sample of it and it had left a sour taste in his mouth.

ها

Brianna roused slowly, aware of great pain. Her eyes were covered with a cool cloth that felt heavenly against the burning sensation and swelling. Moaning softly, she tried to pull the cloth away.

"Nay, Brianna. Be still."

Brianna recognized the soft voice of her friend Mary. How had Mary come to be here? And where exactly was Brianna, anyway? Frowning brought more pain. The last thing she could remember was Edward's fierce rage raining all around her.

"What happened?" Brianna hardly recognized the croaking voice as her own. "Where am I?"

"Shhh, Brie. Don't talk. You will only cause yourself more pain."

Mary placed a chalice against her lips. "Drink this. It will help you sleep."

The cool liquid felt wonderful sliding down her parched throat, but Brianna gagged at its bitter aftertaste.

"What is it?"

Mary chuckled. "One of Alfred's potions."

Brianna slid her hand along the bed until it found Mary's. "Tell me."

Mary was silent for a moment, but then she slowly related all that had transpired since Garek had come to the castle. By the time she had finished, Brianna was already asleep.

ها

When Garek looked in a little later, he found Mary bent over the bed, silently weeping. His heart went out to her.

Crossing to the bed, he looked down at Brianna's battered face and something within him seemed to jump into burning life. He felt angrier than he could ever remember feeling. Would those gentle eyes ever be the same again? Would they ever see the world with the same innocence he had witnessed in them before?

His hand brushed gently against the hair framing Brianna's face. He softly stroked the bruised cheek that was now turning a greenish yellow along the edges.

When his eyes went back to Mary, he found her watching him.

"My men have need of food. I will sit with the girl for now."

Reluctantly, Mary rose to her feet. "Yea, milord."

When she had left, Garek took the stool beside the bed; the stool creaked alarmingly at his weight. He placed Brianna's small hand into his own, comparing hers to his, palm against palm. Hers seemed little more than a child's. How had she survived such a savage beating?

Laying her hand back on the bed, he took the time to study her. He owed this girl his life. He remembered what she had looked like before the beating: brown hair hung almost to her waist in soft, tight ringlets; her skin was pale, unlike most peasant women. Briefly, he wondered why this was so.

Unlike the girl Mary, Brianna was no beauty. For one thing, she was so thin. But there was something compelling about her. As for size, she barely reached to his own heart, although he knew he was a tall man. She seemed so tiny, and almost frail.

His eyes came back to hers and found them open and watching him. Startled, he sat back.

"How fare you?" he asked softly.

"I am well, milord."

Her swollen lips twisted slightly when she spoke.

"It was your brother, was it not?"

Brianna hesitated. Even through a haze of pain she could see the fierce storminess of his cold gray eyes. The man was bent on violence.

"Brianna," he told her, mistaking her hesitation. "You need not fear your brother anymore. Bolson is bringing him here, then I will have him flogged and thrown into the cellar below until I can decide what to do with him."

"Nay! Milord, please! Do not do such a thing."

Confused, Garek stared at her angrily. "What say you, girl? The man almost killed you, and you would not have me do the same to him?"

"God will have vengeance on whom He will have vengeance. It is not for us to usurp His will."

The ragged voice brought Garek's face closer to the battered one on the pillow. Raring back, he rose to his feet.

"I know not of God, but I know plenty of vengeance. You will not stay my hand in this matter. Monsieur Edward will feel my wrath upon the morrow."

"Please. . ."

Garek left the room, slamming the heavy door behind him. He took the stone steps two at a time, his anger churning.

What manner of woman is this, who could be so abused and not seek vengeance? She pleaded for a man's life when he thought not of hers. Again remembering her condition on the road, he gritted his teeth in fury.

He never in his life had treated anyone that way, but the desire to abuse that villein almost overcame his reason.

When he entered the main hall on the ground level, he found his men seated around the room on benches, filling their stomachs with food they had brought with them. Gaylan seemed to have produced trestle tables from somewhere, but Garek was too upset to question the boy about it right now.

He poured himself a cup of ale, taking a long draught. Dark images of what he would like to do to Brianna's brother flitted in and out of his head. Soft blue eyes entered his thoughts, begging for his mercy.

"Aargh!" Slamming his chalice on the table, he stared angrily at the brew that spilled over the side. Bolson came from the other end of the great room.

"Garek?"

"What of the villein?"

"He is below, in the cellar, as you commanded."

"I will speak with him," Garek told the knight coldly. Turning, he strode from the room bent on getting answers to his questions.

Bolson was close behind him. "What will you do?"

"What I will."

The arrogance of the statement went unchecked by his colleague. As lord of this manor, Garek had the right to mete out justice any way he desired.

Lifting a torch from the bracket in the wall, Bolson descended the stairs ahead of Garek. They found Edward huddled in a corner, struggling with the chains on his wrists that Bolson had pegged into the walls of the log structure.

Garek glared at the quivering mass of manhood before him, and although there was little light, Garek had no trouble seeing the man's eyes glittering with hatred and fear.

"You are responsible for your sister's injuries, are you not?" Garek demanded.

At first Edward refused to answer, but then something within him seemed to snap and he lunged to his feet. "Yea! And had I to do it again, I would make sure the traitor never lived to see the light of another day."

A tick grew in Garek's cheek, and he answered Edward softly. "But you will never again have that opportunity, for it is doubtful whether you will see many more days yourself."

Edward said nothing, glaring his hatred at the despised Norman.

"We had a hard time finding him," Bolson told Garek, humor in his voice. "It would seem the men of this fief are from some common ancestor. With those scruffy beards and long hair, they all look the same."

"Yea," Garek agreed. "Perhaps it is the way of these cowards so that no man can put a face to an enemy."

Although Edward continued to glare belligerently, he remained quiet until Garek's slow smile spread across his face and he told the knight at his side, "Shear him."

A bellow of rage followed Garek as he left the cellar, still smiling.

⋇

Climbing the steps, Garek stopped outside the master's chamber. He hesitated before he opened the door and went inside.

Mary rose to her feet, clearly relieved to see him.

"Milord, I cannot settle her down. She will injure herself more if she keeps on this way. She keeps begging to speak with you."

Garek glanced at Brianna. "Leave us."

He watched the maid leave the room before turning to Brianna. He was almost sure what was on her mind.

"Milord," her voice quavered. "What will you do with Edward?"

His eyes avoided hers. "I have not decided."

He heard her move and turned her way. She was trying to sit up. Alarmed, he went quickly to stop her.

"Be still, you foolish girl. Are you trying to finish what your dolt of a brother began?"

He gently pushed her back against the furs, and sat next to her on the bed. "Be still, Brianna," he told her softly. "I will not kill your brother." The promise came easily to his lips, but the will to abide by it was not so easily accomplished.

"I beg you have mercy on him."

Garek felt the anger beginning to rise again. "Listen to me well, maid. On the morrow, yea, even at morningtide, twenty lashes will fall upon the scoundrel's back. My hand will not be stayed in this. It is something that must be done so that others will know the folly of such actions. Do you understand?"

Brianna turned her head away. A small sniffle escaped as a lone tear wound its way down her cheek.

"Brianna?"

"Yea, lord, I understand, but it sits ill with me that I am the cause of another's pain."

"Would that your brother had felt the same." The hardness of his tone left Brianna in no doubt of his feelings.

Garek watched her uneasily, not sure how to assuage her feelings of guilt. What had she to feel guilty about? That rogue below had brought this on himself.

"Why did he beat you, Brianna?"

She wouldn't answer. He could see her shoulders tense.

"Answer me, girl," he commanded softly.

For a long time there was silence in the room. Finally she turned back to him. "It was because you are Norman. When he found I had warned you, he was. . .he was very angry."

Garek smiled, but there was no amusement in his eyes. "So, I am the cause of your misfortune."

Quickly she turned to him, flinching as the pain shot through her body. "Nay, milord. We all answer for our own actions."

"That is what I have been trying to tell you," he argued gently. "Your brother's pain will be his own."

Brianna turned her head toward the wall. Her voice came back, low and quiet. "You do not understand."

Getting up, Garek went to the window and stared up at the moon. It was less full than last night, but still the bright orb bathed the landscape in light. The hour must be late.

"I knew how much my brother hated the Normans," Brianna told him. "I. . .I should have been more sensitive to his feelings."

Garek snorted. "The man has no feelings."

"It is not true, milord. Edward was not always this way."

Surprised at her ready defense, Garek studied her from across the room.

"Then what, pray tell, changed him? What could possibly change a man that much?"

"He was married and had a beautiful daughter. They were all very happy together."

"And?"

Her voice lowered to a husky whisper. "They were both

killed by Norman knights, but not before. . .before. . ."

She stopped, unable to go on. Closing her eyes against the memory of that pain, Brianna gave a little hiccuping sob.

Garek crossed to the bed and stared down at the small figure in it. Sitting on the side of the bed, he took her hand gently in his.

"Others have suffered such misfortunes without becoming monsters."

"They made him watch."

Sudden sympathy stirred in Garek's chest for the man he had hitherto considered nothing but a dog. If it had been Garek's family, what would he have done? By his sword, he would have seen them all slain!

"At least your brother has experienced such a love," Garek told her. "He should be thankful for that. . ." His voice suddenly hardened. "But I will not have him take his vengeance out on you."

Rising, he left the room. He leaned against the wall outside the chamber. Blowing softly through his lips, he raised his eyes heavenward. What horror, war. Why did human beings have to inflict such atrocities against their fellow human beings?

Had it been his family, he would have wanted vengeance, also. But to take it out on a small, helpless female! And his own sister at that.

A sudden thought came to him. A grin spread across his face as he contemplated the idea. Yea, that was the answer.

"Come with me, Bolson," he commanded as he passed the great room heading for the stairs that led to the cellar. Bolson dropped his leg of boar on the trencher and quickly followed his lord.

Edward sat huddled in the corner, glaring hatred. Garek stood before him, tall and angry.

"On the morrow, man, you will have your chance at vengeance. Yea, on the morrow you and I will have a contest.

Think on it this night and let your hatred burn and give you strength, for by all that is holy, it will be your last chance."

The hostility in Edward's eyes was suddenly replaced by fear. His face grew pale and sweat erupted on his forehead as he contemplated Garek's words. "Yea, sir knight," he spat. "What is it to you to kill another lowly Saxon?"

The quietness of Garek's voice sent shivers down even Bolson's back.

"It is nothing to me."

# three

Garek picked his way down the long, dark, mist-enshrouded corridor. At the far end of the corridor he could see a light. Desperate to escape the gloom, he strode quickly in that direction, but the faster he walked, the farther away the light seemed to be.

A hand reached out to him from the shadows, grasping at his mantle. Startled, he turned, only to be confronted by a headless body.

Yelling, he flung the hand away from him only to find it replaced by another, and then another. Moans echoed along the corridor, cries of pain that grew louder as he tried to flee.

Each corpse was bent on one purpose: reaching Garek. They cried out in plaintive chorus, moaning eerily.

"You killed me! You killed me!"

Gritting his teeth, Garek turned and fled in the opposite direction, but whichever way he turned, the light was always there ahead of him, just out of reach.

Suddenly a woman stood before him, her mocking laughter reaching him across the dark abyss that had riven the ground before his feet. Her golden hair blazed forth from the light that spilled behind her, her blue eyes shooting sparks of fire.

He turned to run again, only to find himself confronted by the villein he had so recently visited. The man's evil grin reached out to him.

Behind the man, the light grew brighter. Garek had to get to the light. His very survival depended on it, and he knew there was only one way through.

Drawing his sword, Garek motioned to the villein to move aside. The man only laughed harder.

"Begone, I say! I do not want to have to slay you!"

The words echoed around and around the chamber: Slay you! Slay you!

Lifting his sword, he brought it down in a flashing arc, slicing into the body before him. As the body dropped slowly to the floor, it changed before Garek's eyes. Evil eyes changed to a soft blue. The taunting face became a serene, gentle one, the eyes closing slowly as the girl before him stared in horror.

"Nay!"

Garek came upright in bed, the sweat pouring from his body even though the room was freezing cold. He was alone in the great hall, his knights and their squires having chosen the stables as their bedrooms. Even Gaylan chose to sleep in the kitchen, the only other available rooms being those on the floor above—for the lord of the manor.

He shoved the wolf pelts aside and climbed from the mat half-clothed.

Crossing the room, he gave little heed to the chill of the planks beneath his feet. He lifted a wineskin from a table and drank heavily, shivering as the cold liquid tore its way through his body. Throwing the skin down, he turned back to the bed.

Garek sat down, brushing his hands tiredly across his face. Slowly, he lay back against the furs.

It was the same every night. Each time he closed his eyes, faces of the dead rose up to haunt him, among them his wife.

Groaning, he closed his eyes and tried to remember. This time it had been different. Whereas before he had only been surrounded by darkness, this time he could see a light.

What had the villein to do with his dreams? He had first encountered the man only two nights ago, and now the man was part and parcel of Garek's nighttime musings.

He shuddered as he remembered the face with the soft blue eyes. Brianna. She had been the source of the light. Was God trying to tell him something? More likely, his own guilty conscience and too much ale had caused his slumber to be so interrupted.

Garek got up again and crossed to the hearth in the middle of the room. The fire had almost died out by now. Throwing on some kindling, Garek gave thought to what was about to transpire.

The flame caught and soon the chill eased in the chamber, although the smoke thickened around him, making his eyes sting. Garek decided he'd had enough sleep for one night. It couldn't be long until morning.

Pulling on a soft leather tunic over the chausses covering his legs, he went to the window and looked out. Already the faint fingers of dawn were streaking across the eastern sky.

Below him in the courtyard he could see signs of activity. Bolson was awake and making ready for the contest to come.

Sighing, Garek turned away. How was he to get out of this mess he had made for himself? He could have hanged the villein from the nearest tree. But somehow, Garek knew without a doubt that soft blue eyes would haunt him the rest of his life if he did so.

He pulled on his boots and made his way to the lord's chamber. Gently he opened the door and peered inside.

Brianna rested peacefully on the bed, her eyes closed in sweet repose. Mary lay on a pallet next to the great bed, her even breathing telling Garek that she, too, was fast asleep.

Closing the door, he made his way down the stairs and crossed to the table at the end of the main hall. He slid into a chair, dropping his head upon his hands.

"My lord?"

Startled, Garek glanced up at young Gaylan standing beside his chair.

"I did not hear you come in," he told the boy. "What is it you wish?"

"Will you break the fast, my lord? There is not much provender left until we finish unpacking the supplies, but I will see what I can find. . . ."

Garek shook his head. "Nay. Bring me only a chalice of ale."

Gaylan hesitated. "There is cool milk, if you would rather."

Feeling the queasy turn of his stomach, Garek decided he would rather have the latter.

"Yea, bring me a cup."

Garek watched the boy leave the room, entering the cooking chamber beyond. *He's a good lad. There must be something I can do to help the boy's position—perhaps make him a page and help him begin a journey toward knighthood.* He would give it some thought.

There were so many things to think about, not least of which was what to do about Brianna's brother. He knew whatever he decided, he had to protect Brianna from him. *The problem is, the foolish girl seems to have a fondness for the dolt.*

Women! There was no understanding them. No reasoning with them. Especially when they took some notion into their heads. . .or hearts.

Bolson entered the room, crossing to Garek's side.

"Everything is ready." He hesitated. "Will you really kill the man?"

Garek blew out through his lips, slanting his friend a look as he did so. "If you can think of another way to protect the wench from the fool, I will gladly listen."

Bolson pinched his lips together with his fingers, studying Garek thoughtfully. "Perhaps you could send him away."

"And what is to prevent him from returning and wreaking more havoc upon us?"

Grinning, Bolson drew a bench forward and sat. "Perhaps Anton could keep him occupied in France," he suggested, referring to Garek's cousin, who was notoriously anti-English.

Garek looked at his knight askance. "Pray tell, why this concern for a Saxon life?"

Bolson sobered. "I do not like killing, my liege. If there is another way, I would use it. The reason for such an act in this case is quite understandable, yet it would seem the lesser of two evils to let the man live."

"Has your heart turned to England, Sir Bolson?"

Affronted, the blond knight rose to his feet, his blue eyes flashing in anger. "Nay! It is not so!"

A sparkle in Garek's eyes belied the seriousness of his words. "Then pray tell, Sir Bolson, why would you choose to inflict such a man upon my kinsmen? What have the Normans ever done to deserve such a reward?"

Seeing the jest of his words, Bolson relaxed. "It is only that I thought our kind might better be able to teach the oaf some manners."

The sparkle grew as Garek considered the suggestion. "Yea," he said softly. "You just may have the right idea."

Rising from the table, Garek clasped his friend's forearm with his hand. "Yea, Bolson. Let us make haste to secure this day and this fief."

Laughing, the two friends left the room, watched by a bemused Gaylan who was holding a chalice of milk.

❧

Serin lifted the huge broadsword and handed it to Edward. The man backed away as though the instrument were an asp about to strike.

Garek drew his own sword from its scabbard and stood facing the villein. An eyebrow winged its way upward in amusement.

"What, ho, Edward? Are you refusing the challenge?"

Garek grinned as the man glared back at him, rubbing his now clean-shaven face.

"I am no knight trained to do battle. Neither am I foolish enough to fight one."

Garek rested the point of his sword in the dirt, leaning upon the hilt. "I agree you are not trained to do battle, but you have learned the act well." His voice grew cold. "Especially upon women and unsuspecting travelers. As to the second point, I must disagree, for a bigger fool I have yet to meet."

Edward trembled with his wrath, and no little amount of fear. His mouth opened, then closed. Garek continued.

"These many years you have longed to wreak vengeance on the Normans, yet now your opportunity has arisen and you refuse the honor. I say that is very foolish."

"I will not fight you," Edward declared. "It would not be a fair fight. You are far larger than me and greatly exceed my abilities."

"Perhaps you would prefer someone more like your sister?" Garek paused as if considering the idea, his lips pursed upward. "Agreed."

He snapped his fingers and a young man came forward. He wore no mail, nor any of the accouterments of a knight.

Garek handed his sword to the lad, who was obviously no more than eighteen. Though the boy was slight of build, he hefted the sword easily.

"Devon, will you fight this. . .this gentleman?"

Short blond hair bobbed as the boy nodded. "Aye, milord. It will be my pleasure."

Garek turned back to Edward. "Devon is training to be a knight, true, but he is not one yet. And since he is but a lad I thought perhaps you would have less fear."

Although his face flushed at the sneer in Garek's voice, Edward refused to lift his sword. Garek turned to him in anger.

"You have a choice. Fight, or be sent to Normandy where you will swear allegiance to William and be made a serf in the fief of my cousin."

Edward's eyes grew large. They went from Garek to Devon, and back again. He swallowed hard, trying to decide.

"Choose!" Garek bellowed. "I grow weary of the wait."

"And if I fight?"

Garek's demeanor grew cold as he studied the man. Edward

was not a small man and at some time must have been considered handsome. The years and circumstances had taken their toll and left him with a bitter twist to his lips. Still, Garek had no doubt of the outcome should he decide to fight Devon.

"Should you win the day, you will be set free."

"And I may leave this manor?"

Garek grinned at Devon, who grinned back. "Oh, yea, you may leave."

Still Edward hesitated, appearing very much the coward. Garek decided to help him make up his mind. He walked across the courtyard, drawing Bolson's sword from its scabbard. Turning, he walked back to where Devon waited. Facing the boy, Garek smiled.

"To arms, Devon."

Grinning, the boy hefted his own sword. In one quick move he sliced down and to the left, taking Garek by surprise. Garek lifted his sword in time to turn the blow to the side. Sword rang against sword.

In the chamber above, Brianna flinched at the clash of steel against steel. Mary leaned out over the sill, watching the conflict below. So absorbed was she, she failed to notice Brianna slowly climbing from the bed. Only when the dark-haired girl joined her did Mary protest.

"Brianna! Get back in bed!"

"Nay," she whispered hoarsely. "I will see this out."

They both watched as Devon and Garek continued their sport. The boy was well skilled, though small of stature, and was a fair match for the older man.

Even from this distance Brianna could tell that Garek held back so as not to harm the boy accidentally. She also could see that Edward's face had grown pale.

"Enough!" Garek's voice rang louder than the blade, and Devon dropped his sword to his side.

Turning, Garek fixed Edward with a look. "Your decision?"

Edward dropped his sword. He knew he was no match for

the boy, though he exceeded him in weight. Perhaps life in a French court would not be such an unhappy experience. With enough cunning, he might even gain the lord's ear.

"Wise choice," Garek told him.

Brianna sagged back against the wall in relief. Concerned, Mary edged her toward the bed.

"I told you, did I not? Now get back into bed, for heaven's sake! It is not my wont to be flayed if milord finds you sprawled out in the rushes."

Brianna had no more than lain down before her eyes closed in sleep.

❧

When Brianna opened her eyes again, daylight was waning. Garek sat in a chair by her bed, his head nodding to the side. Brianna smiled at the innocent picture he made.

How could one who could wield a sword and mete out justice so efficiently look so innocent?

She took time to study him, noticing that he had removed the stubble of several days growth from his face. Brianna had a hard time adjusting to this Norman custom of appearance, but she found it rather appealing. He had trimmed his hair as well. It framed his face, causing the scar on his forehead to stand out more clearly.

Brianna acknowledged that he was a fine figure of a man. Who could deny it? But she sensed in him a restlessness and an anger that seemed unquenchable. How she could know this after such short acquaintance she was unsure, but know it she did.

She blinked in surprise when his eyes suddenly opened, staring into hers. Relief was quickly disguised behind a bland mask.

"It is eventide, damsel. We thought perhaps you would sleep the night away."

She didn't return his smile. "What of Edward?"

Mary had told Garek that they had witnessed the morning's

encounter from the window, but Garek knew they were unaware of any words that were spoken, the distance being too great.

Garek leaned forward, bringing his face close to Brianna's. He raised a finger and gently stroked the swollen bruise on her cheek.

"I have sent him from England, to my cousin in Normandy. Perhaps he will learn to fight men instead of women." His voice was unusually soft as his eyes slowly roved over her face.

"Poor Edward," Brianna sighed.

Garek rose to his feet, angry at the girl's continued championing of such a worm as Edward.

"Waste not your pity on Edward. Men like him always find a way to turn disfavor to their advantage." He crossed to the window, staring out at the gathering darkness.

The torch light flickered, making shadows dance across the floor. The warmth seemed to reach out and touch Garek and he found himself oddly content.

"Brianna," he asked. "Are you familiar with this shire?"

She watched him carefully, wondering at his sudden change of subject.

"Yea, my lord. I have lived here since I was but six years of age."

Garek grinned, throwing her a look over his shoulder. "And how long ago was that? Nine years? Ten?"

Blushing, Brianna turned her head away from him. "My lord, you jest."

Surprised, Garek crossed the room to her side. "What is your age?"

The color deepened on Brianna's cheeks. "I am well past marrying age, my lord. I am a score plus six."

Garek couldn't believe his ears. This little thing twenty-six years old? Surely not.

"You are making a jest," he scoffed.

Brianna turned back to him, her eyes suddenly curious.

"Truly you believed I was but six years plus ten?"

"Yea." Flustered, his look went from her head to her tiny little feet. "Perhaps your size had something to do with it, but you are. . .there is something. . ."

He found himself unable to go on. How did one explain that women, older women, had an air about them, a lack of innocence that sat hard upon their features?

This girl had the look of one as yet untouched. In truth, she looked more the maid than many much younger girls, though with her face swollen so grotesquely, it was hard to tell. Garek brought them back to a less personal topic of conversation.

"You say you know the shire and its people?"

"Yea."

He seated himself once again. "I have need of someone who can help me learn this land and its people. Would this be acceptable to you?"

Brianna was puzzled. "Milord, what is it you ask of me? Am I not to be sent with Edward?"

"Nay! Never that!" Garek lowered his voice. "You will stay here, at the castle. Mary has need of someone to help her with her chores and my men do not fancy being land serfs."

Brianna tried to smile. "Methinks young Devon would make a fine smithy."

"Yea, he strikes the iron well, but it is better, I think, to have him at my side."

Garek could see the tired droop of Brianna's eyes. He pulled the tray that Mary had fixed across the floor.

"Can you eat, Brianna?"

"I am famished," she told him, eyeing the tray hungrily.

Placing the tray on the bed next to her, Garek tried to help Brianna eat the bread and cheese Mary had brought. A flagon of water was there to quench her thirst.

Raising an eyebrow, Garek smiled at her. "Rather meager fare, but until I have time to make the rounds of the manor and find out the exact state of my affairs, it will have to do.

My men are already complaining, so perhaps I will send them out hunting on the morrow."

"My lord." Brianna halted him as he was about to leave the room. "The folk of this shire are good, hard-working people. They will not cheat you nor do you harm if they are treated with dignity and respect."

Was there a warning in her words? Garek's eyes narrowed. He'd had enough of Saxon treachery to last a lifetime. Even now it sat sorely upon him that he must be lord of this manor. He'd rather be back home in Normandy.

"Make haste in your healing, Brianna. I am in sore need, as I told you, of someone to help me establish this burg."

This time Brianna returned his smile. He closed the door softly behind him.

Mary came later to retrieve the tray. Her eyes were alight, her face flushed. Brianna studied her, wondering what had put her friend in such a fine humor. She didn't have long to wait.

"Sir Bolson asked after you," Mary told her in a breathy voice.

Brianna's lips twitched. "Did he now?"

"Yea," Mary told her, not noticing her friend's twitching lips. "He is a fine man, would you not say so?"

Eyebrows raised, Brianna answered her friend. "In truth, I do not know the man, but if you say it is so, then it must be."

A dreamy look crept over Mary's features. "Yea. Strong. Handsome. Wealthy."

"How do you know he is wealthy?"

Mary flared at the snicker in her friend's voice. "He told me so."

"I see."

Fists on her hips, Mary glared at Brianna. Before she could say anything, a knock at the door interrupted them.

Gaylan pushed open the door slightly. "My lord wishes a word with you, Mary."

All humor fled the girl's face. "Coming."

After she had gone, Brianna stared at the door. Her lips twitched with amusement. *Mary is forever falling in love. The problem is, it never lasts.* The smile drained away. Except for James. He had been killed at the battle of Hastings. It surprised Brianna that Mary would even consider a Norman, especially since they were responsible for the death of her intended and the destruction and ruin of the English countryside.

She sighed. Did Garek du Mor truly believe that she, Brianna, was as young as he said, or was he merely being kind? She had long since given up the idea of marriage and family, since she was considered an old maid and had no dowry.

But now that Edward was being sent away, what was she to do? It was obvious Sir Garek felt sorry for her, probably even felt some kind of obligation since she had saved his life.

Brianna sighed again. It would be nice to be as lovely as Mary and have men constantly throwing flowers at your feet. Mary had only to walk into a room and it became a brighter place.

Settling back against the mattress, she felt a moment's guilt at having routed the lord from his own bed chambers. Still, guilt did not keep her eyes from slowly drifting shut.

When Garek looked in on her later, Brianna's breathing came softly to his ears. Walking across the room, he stared down at her.

"Ho, wench. What have you to do with the light?" he asked softly, studying her sleeping figure several long moments. "If you invade the privacy of my dreams again, could you not make them a little more pleasant?"

A soft murmur answered him and he realized that Brianna was in a dream world of her own. Touching her cheek lightly, Garek smiled down at her.

"Sweet dreams, little Brianna."

Turning, he quickly exited the room.

## four

Days turned into weeks and the time brought healing and change to Brianna's life. No longer did she spend her days toiling relentlessly for a man who was unappreciative. No longer did she go to bed hungry each night.

Garek noticed the changes in the girl, studying her thoughtfully. Her bones no longer protruded from her clothes and a healthy pink tinged her cheeks. The bruises faded, and once again Brianna's skin turned milk white. He knew she could never be considered comely, but there was something about her that arrested one's attention—a peaceful serenity that nothing seemed to mar.

Garek's knights were taken with Mary's loveliness, often fighting over who would be the one to win her favor, but it was Brianna who won their chivalry.

It amused Garek to watch his knights fall all over themselves trying to keep the young maid from lifting heavy platters or lugging huge water buckets. None of them could forget the maid's condition when she had first arrived.

Often Brianna was found sitting with one of his knights, their faces close together as she earnestly exhorted the man on some point. Since Garek could not hear these conversations, he didn't know what was transpiring among his men. It began to irritate him, for she made a point of staying as far from the lord of the manor as possible.

The seasons had changed as well. The dampness from the surrounding swamps had been replaced by bone-biting cold and heavy snows.

Brianna and Mary often sat huddled together in the warm kitchen. Sometimes they would go to the adjacent chamber to spin flax, chatting amiably.

This day they were laughing over some shared joke when suddenly the door was flung open and Garek strode in, carrying a large coffer. He thumped it down in front of the girls, motioning with his hands and speaking to Brianna.

"It was brought with the idea of using them as trade goods. It is yours—both of you. I owe you."

Mary and Brianna stared at him with gaping mouths as he turned and left the room.

Squealing, Mary hurriedly opened the trunk, raring back in surprise at the rich array of gowns nestled therein.

"Oh, Brianna," she breathed.

Brianna slowly lifted out a gown of rich red velvet. Never in her life had she seen anything so lovely. She lifted it to her lap and began stroking the soft fox-fur trim.

Mary looked at the closed door. "What manner of man is he?"

Brianna spoke without thought. "A lonely man, I think."

Hurriedly shoving the gowns back into the trunk, Mary gave a disgusted snort.

"He cannot purchase my favor with such as these."

"Nay, Mary," Brianna answered. "It was only a kindness, I am sure."

Mary was far from satisfied. "Perhaps, but I think the gowns are not worth what may be the price."

Brianna stared down at her own torn and mended gown of rough wool. The softer kirtle she wore beneath was so thin from wear that it did little to alleviate the itch from the outer garment.

With the onset of winter, she was always cold, her worn gown being the only one she owned. The velvet would be warm. But if Mary could not see her way to accept any of the garments, then Brianna felt she must reject them too.

Sadly, Brianna began to lay the dress back into the coffer, folding it ever so gently.

"What are you about, Brianna?"

"If you think it not wise to accept the garments, then neither can I."

Mary stared back at her friend. Her eyes quickly went over the girl's threadbare clothing.

"But, Brianna. It would be all right for you to make use of the dresses."

"How so?"

Biting her lip, Mary was at a loss to explain how she knew that the lord of the manor would expect nothing of Brianna in return for such a favor. He treated Brianna with a gentle courtesy that his knights were quick to follow.

Of course, that was Brianna. Something about Brianna had always encouraged others to see her as a child needing protection.

Mary's eyes grew dark. Except for that blackguard of a brother of hers. She wondered what the new lord would think if he knew the whole truth of Brianna's situation.

Returning her eyes to the coffer, she sighed. Truly the gowns were lovely, and although she was but a servant along with Brianna, it would be pleasant to be so robed. She couldn't deny Brianna this kindness.

Lifting out a gold gown of rich brocade, Mary smiled saucily. "This would surely make the eyes of Sir Bolson pop from his head, would it not?"

Confused, Brianna nodded.

"Take no thought to my rambling lips, Brianna. It is just that I look for false motives in everything these days. Let us enjoy these lovely gowns as the lord has bid us."

"Surely?" Brianna still hesitated.

"Yea."

The two girls hurriedly went through the coffer, dividing the garments between them. When Brianna lay in her own chamber that night, her thoughts were with Garek, who had shown her such a kindness.

In the days that followed, Garek took Brianna with him on his surveys of the countryside. His fief was a large one, and much work would be required to make it profitable.

His decision to take the girl with him proved wise, for she truly did know all the people in the shire. Everyone met her with a glad smile, though their greetings to him were less enthusiastic.

Still, it was not long before the people became accustomed to his presence, and their fear of him grew less and less. This was in no small part due to Brianna's own lack of concern. Her eager acceptance of Garek as lord did much to soothe their misgivings.

Garek himself proved a capable and honest lord. Although the people were required to work three days a week at the castle, the other three days were theirs to maintain their own farms. The seventh day, of course, was a day of rest.

Garek also decided to replace the log palisade with a stone curtain wall, which would require many hours of labor, but in the end it would prove much more secure. The villeins were willing to provide the necessary labor, for well they knew the results of having no protection from invaders.

Garek made Serin his sheriff because the man was well educated and very familiar with figures. Although Serin was a knight, his heart was not in it. He had a mind for learning and chose to use it. This was a blessing for Garek, for there was no one he would consider more trustworthy.

It took weeks for Serin to log each man, woman, child, goat, cow, and other livestock into his books. Again Brianna proved an invaluable ally.

Before long, Garek had the castle fully manned with servants, and serfs began tilling the land in preparation for the spring planting. Others honed scythes and plows and mended harnesses. Everywhere, signs of activity proclaimed the people's willingness to put war behind them.

Word had come to Garek that William had returned to England to defeat an insurrection by a small band of deposed English lords who had aligned themselves with several rebellious lords from Flanders.

Atheling Edward had escaped William's custody and had joined forces with Scottish kings in the north. William himself would lead the forces from Normandy, seeking to stop them.

When Garek offered to join the battle, William bade him remain where he was to protect the area from raiders sweeping across the country.

Garek chafed at his inactivity, knowing full well the rebelliousness of the English. Bolson smiled in sympathy.

"We all wish we could be on our way, Garek. But the king's reasoning is sound. It will take many men to bring this country back to prosperity, and dead men can do naught."

"Aye, but still it goads me."

Brianna entered the room carrying a trencher of roast deer. The inviting smell brought others to the table as she set about making ready a meal for the men.

Garek again noticed how well the maid now filled out her clothes. The gowns he had given her had been put to good use, though Brianna had a tendency to choose the less elaborate dresses. Still, Garek couldn't fault her taste. The gowns gave her the appearance of being a genteel lady, rather than the servant she was.

Mary, entering behind her, was entirely different, he knew. She chose the brightest, most daring ensembles, and her flirtatious manner brought many a hearty whack upon her backside.

The contrast between the two was amazing. Garek shook his head. As he had often said, there was no understanding women.

Brianna set a cup of ale before Garek, her eyes lowered demurely. Stepping back, she kept her head bowed.

"Is there anything else, my lord?"

What was there about this girl that soothed his very soul? He could be in the foulest mood and she had only to enter the room to send his anger fleeing. Her presence was a calming balm.

Taking her by the wrist, he gently pushed her onto the bench next to his chair.

"Aye. Sit and eat."

Her eyelids opened wide at this, and she started to rise; his raised eyebrows made her sit again.

"It is not proper, milord. A servant's place is not at the table with the lord."

Irritated at having caused all eyes to turn his way, Garek lifted his ale and took a hearty swig. "A servant's place is where the lord so deems. Now eat."

Exchanging glances with Mary, Brianna shrugged her shoulders. Mary's eyes were alight with laughter, and something Brianna could not name. She brought Brianna a boat of bread from which to eat her meal, grinning as she laid it before her.

Garek returned to his meal and never again turned Brianna's way. Thoroughly confused, she picked at the meat and bread. She couldn't relax, knowing that Mary and the other servants were doing the work she should be doing.

When the meal was finished, Brianna excused herself to help Mary in the kitchen. Garek allowed her to leave without so much as glancing her way.

From that day forward, Garek expected Brianna to sit at his side during the evening meal. Brianna didn't like it, but there was nothing she could do. She grew aggravated at Mary's knowing glances.

"He fancies you," Mary told her.

"Have you lost all reason?"

"Nay," Mary told her confidently. "I have seen the way he watches you. Does he not bid you stay close by his side when he is here at the castle? And does he not take you with him when he does his rounds of the shire?"

Brianna knew Mary was right about Garek wanting her by his side, but she also knew there was another reason besides fancy that caused Garek to seek her out. She felt it in the dark, brooding look of his eyes.

Brianna soon found out the reason for his interest. It was several days later, long past midnight, when Brianna made her way up the cold stone steps to her chamber above.

Alfred had asked her help tending a child ill with fever. The time had dragged by until, finally, just before midnight, the fever broke. The walk from the village had been long and cold. In the darkness, Brianna had shivered at the rustlings along the wayside. She had known it was probably the wind, but she'd shuddered with apprehension nonetheless.

Brianna wearily made her way to the door of her chamber, adjacent to Garek's. She was brought up short by a shout from the lord's chamber. Eyes wide with fright, she stared at the closed door separating her from the man within.

A moment later the door swung open and Garek stood on its threshold, wearing a hastily donned tunic over his chausses.

When he saw Brianna, his face relaxed. "I would have a word with you."

Brianna looked beyond him inside the room. Nothing moved. Her eyes searched Garek's.

"A nightmare, milord?"

"Aye."

Still, she hesitated to enter his room as he moved aside and motioned her in. Recognizing her reluctance, Garek took her impatiently by the arm and, turning her around, marched her down the stairs to the great hall below.

"Sit," he commanded, and Brianna took a seat on the stool beside the now cold hearth. Garek lit one torch on the wall and Brianna could see his face twisted with some nameless worry.

Brianna tried to stem the trembling of her hands by twisting

them in her lap. She could see sweat beading on Garek's forehead, even though the room was barely above freezing. He
truly seemed frightened, which surprised her. A man such as
he—strong and courageous. What had he to fear?

"I want to share my dream with you," he finally told her,
seating himself across from her. "Perhaps you can explain it
to me."

Brianna was surprised. "I am no prophet."

"I know not of prophets," he told her, "only dreams."

He related his nightmare to her. It was similar to the others
he'd had. The only difference in them was that instead of
striking down Edward and Edward then transforming into
Brianna, Brianna was now alone. As the shadows had reached
for him, he had reached for the light. He could never quite
reach it, but it drew ever closer and he knew the light came
from Brianna.

When he finished, Brianna stared at him, unsure what to
say.

"It would seem to me that your guilt drives your dreams,"
she finally told him.

"Of what guilt do you speak?"

"From what you have told me, guilt over the taking of other
lives."

Garek snorted. "I killed my first man when I was but a
score years old. Since that time I have taken many lives,
though only in defense of my king. My dreams started only
three years ago." He studied her. "But what have you to do
with the light? I never saw the light in my dreams until I met
you."

Brianna turned her face from him. "Perhaps it is the Lord
Jesus Christ that is the true light. Perhaps you see Him in me,
and He is calling for you."

Garek's eyes narrowed. "What say you?"

"The Lord lives in me. He has promised this from the
beginning. Any light that is in me surely comes from Him, for

I have no light of my own."

"You speak of prophets and promises. What can you know of such things? Only the priests have the knowledge of God."

Brianna smiled, though her eyes were serious. "When I first came to this shire, it was as a child. My mother died giving me birth, and my father decided to come back to this shire of his childhood. He had gone to Normandy when he was younger and wished to come home. I was but six when he decided this."

"And Edward?" Garek asked softly.

"Edward was a child of my father's first marriage. My father was two score and ten when he married my mother. She was but eighteen."

Brianna hesitated to go on. The story was painful to her even after all of these years. Garek sat waiting for her to continue. Taking a deep breath, she went on.

"When we arrived here, my father sent me to the convent." She nodded her head toward the window. "He. . .he could not bear the sight of me. It was years before I learned the reason why."

Garek was intrigued. "And that was. . . ?"

Brianna's voice was so soft, Garek had to strain to hear.

"I was not my father's daughter."

Shocked, Garek leaned back in his seat. It was the way of women, was it not? An unfaithful lot, never abiding by their vows. He knew this from experience. He waited for her to continue, not daring to interrupt.

"My father was a man for hire. His arms went to those who would pay the highest price. He was often away, and he and my mother had not married for love."

"That is no excuse. A vow is a vow," Garek told her coldly.

Surprised at his anger, Brianna plumbed the depths of his cold gray gaze.

"True. I am not trying to excuse her, only to state a truth."

Brianna got up and strolled to the window. The darkness

was absolute, the new moon giving no light.

"The nuns in the convent raised me until. . .until Edward's family was killed and he had need of someone to help at the farm. I was a score years old plus one when I left the sanctuary of the convent. It was the nuns who taught me of Jesus."

Everything fell into place for Garek. Brianna's innocence and her gentle ways, her ability to read and write.

"I have asked for absolution," he told her angrily. "I paid a high price to the priests, but it does not take the dreams away."

Brianna turned her face to him. "You cannot be granted absolution from men. It must come from God."

Puzzled, he got up and crossed the room to stand beside her. "Then what can I do? How can I receive absolution from God?"

"You must ask," she told him. "And renounce your sins."

"Of what sins do you speak? I am a soldier under the authority of the king. It is not so simple. . ."

"I speak not of your occupation, but of your heart. King David was a man who slew tens of thousands of men, and yet the holy Scriptures teach that he was a man after God's own heart."

"Truly? The holy Word says this?"

"Yea. It was not that David had a blood lust, but only that he defended his people. There is no guilt in such a thing."

Garek watched the shadows dance across Brianna's face in the light of the flickering torch. He yearned for something he could not put a name to.

Reaching out, he lifted a lock of her curly brown hair, stroking it between his fingers. She watched him, her eyes wide.

"There is more, Garek, is there not? Something you have kept from me?"

Surprised at her use of his given name, he stilled. He abruptly dropped her hair from his fingers. "Why do you ask such a thing?"

She said nothing, waiting for him to continue. He returned to his seat, throwing himself upon the stool that creaked alarmingly under his weight. Brianna followed him, seating herself again on her stool. Minutes went by and still he said nothing.

Brianna was growing weary, realizing that several hours had passed since she had entered the keep. As tired as she was, she remained stoically seated upon the stool, waiting for him to speak.

When he turned to her, there was anguish in his eyes.

"I killed my wife."

## five

The silence in the room grew uncomfortably long. Slowly Garek lifted his head, brushing his face with his hands. The torch had begun to fail and the room had grown darker, casting his face in shadows.

Brianna waited for him to continue, knowing he wasn't finished with what he had to say. She struggled to think of this gentle, caring man she had come to know quite well, as a monster who could slay his wife.

Finally he spoke, his face drawn tight with remembered pain.

"I was away much of the time. Elizabeth was young, beautiful, full of life. I have learned since that beauty often hides an evil heart."

He looked her way, studying her in the dim light. Brianna squirmed under his scrutiny, wondering what he was thinking.

"She married me, I think, for my position in Duke William's court." Sighing, he brushed his hands through his hair, leaving it in disarray. The room was now colder, and his breath was visible as he spoke. Brianna shivered, but Garek seemed oblivious.

"While I was away on the duke's business, it seems my wife found ways to keep herself occupied—one of them being a soldier in the duke's army. They decided to run away together, back to his home in Flanders. It was not expected that I would return as soon as I did."

Finally, Garek noticed Brianna's shivering form huddled against the room's creeping cold. He crossed the room to retrieve a fur pelt from a pallet in the corner and wrapped it snugly around Brianna. Ignoring her thankful look, he sank back on his stool, his eyes taking on a distant look.

"I returned the very day they fled. It took me some time to sort out the situation, but when I did, I went after them." His eyes darkened to obsidian, the flames of the torch reflected in their depths. The words began to flow again; it was as though now that the door had been opened, nothing could keep them from flooding forth.

"I caught up with them five miles outside the city. I can still see the look of horror on Elizabeth's face when she spotted me behind them. Perhaps I looked like the Devil himself, for truly I meant to kill them both as soon as I caught them."

He stopped, reliving that day in his mind. Brianna's soft voice brought his eyes back to where she sat on the stool before him. The only outward sign of her feelings was the slight tremble of her lips.

"You say you killed them?"

He continued to stare at her as though she were his only link with sanity. "They saw me coming and her. . .her lover spurred the horses into a run." Garek snorted. "They thought their wagon could outdistance my steed. Instead, the wagon careened from one side of the road to the other, finally turning over with them beneath." He finished softly, "They were dead when I reached them."

"But Garek," Brianna cried. "It was no fault of yours."

He glared angrily back at her. "It was my fault they fled. It was my fault they were together in the first place. It was my fault they died, for if not for the wagon, I surely would have slain them."

Brianna got up and kneeled before him, earnestly pleading with her eyes.

"You cannot know that for a certain."

"Yea," he snarled angrily. "I can."

Brianna shook her head, her dark curls bobbing in her agitation. "It is not like the man I have come to know. I cannot believe you would have done such a thing."

Looking down at her kneeling before him, Garek knew suddenly what his other knights sought from this maid. Her faith made him want to stand a little straighter, be the man she thought he was. Yea, she made him feel like a man, not just a king's pawn.

He reached out, cupping her chin in his hand. His eyes found hers, and held. Though she didn't pull away, he could see her eyes grow distant. Regardless of what she said, she didn't trust him, he was sure. He dropped his hand and sat back.

Brianna felt herself relax again. Every time Garek touched her, she felt things she didn't understand. He frightened her in ways she couldn't fathom, but she didn't fear the man himself. He had been nothing but kind to her.

She rose to her feet, looking down at Garek's bent head. "God kept you from committing such a sin. You should be thankful."

Garek rose swiftly to his feet and Brianna stepped back. He barely glanced her way before turning to pace to and fro in the chamber.

"It is no sin to slay a cheating wife!"

"If you believed that to be so, you would not feel such guilt."

"You spoke to me once before of guilt. Is it the guilt of soldiers slain, or an unfaithful spouse?"

"You said the dreams started but three years past?"

"Aye!" Garek shoved his large hands through his rumpled hair.

"And was that the time that your wife. . .that she died?"

Nodding, Garek's gaze raked her face. "You think the two are connected? Is it God's way of punishing me for the sin I have committed?"

Brianna's eyes softened. "Nay. Perhaps it is God's way of trying to gain your attention. You must forgive your wife and yourself so that God can forgive you."

Garek was growing angrier. "What say you? It is not an easy matter to forgive unfaithfulness."

"God knows that, Garek. He speaks of it all through His holy Word." With some hesitation, Brianna crossed to his side. She had to make him see. "God's chosen people were continually unfaithful to Him throughout history. Only when they were in trouble would they remember Him and call on Him to save them."

"I was always faithful to my wife. My vows were for life."

"But did you not also swear fealty to your king and to God Himself?" Brianna asked him.

"Yea, and I have not been unfaithful to either."

Frustrated, Brianna tried to make him see himself in another way. "And was it God you served when you looted and killed and. . .and other such things?"

His lips twitched in sudden amusement. "I have never raped a woman, Brianna. I have never had to."

Face red, Brianna held her ground. "Fornication is as much a sin as adultery. Both are deserving of death in the Lord's eyes."

"I have told you before, I am a knight in the king's service. I am not free to choose where and when I go nor what I do. Death is a part of my duties."

"Yea, Garek," she told him, touching his arm. "But it is of forgiveness I speak. You must forgive yourself so that God can forgive you too."

Garek took her hand and lifted it to his lips, touching her fingers briefly with his kiss. She drew her breath in sharply. His eyes devoured hers as he attempted to absorb what she was trying to say. His mind was fogged by exhaustion, and he could see the tired droop of Brianna's shoulders.

Bending his head, he brought his lips softly against hers. "Go to bed, Brianna," he told her.

Needing no other bidding, she fled.

❧

A shout from the watchtower sent Brianna and Mary to the

doorway leading to the courtyard below. Loud words from the gatehouse indicated the gatekeeper knew the rider below, and eventually the drawbridge was lowered, allowing the horseman to proceed.

Garek had taken to keeping the drawbridge raised after bands of raiders started raiding in the shire. Even now Garek and his men rode in search of the marauders.

The rider pulled up at the steps leading to the manor, doffing his helm as he appraised the two maidens standing before him. A slow grin spread across his face, his green eyes growing lighter as they gained a merry sparkle.

"Forsooth, had I known such a welcome would await me, I would have hastened instead of dawdling, as is my wont."

Brianna smiled slightly, recognizing the young man's words as the foolery they were intended to be. The symbols on his shield proclaimed him a knight, and Brianna wondered what had brought the young man to their shire.

Before she could ask, Mary pranced down the stairs and stood at the foot of the man's steed. Her bright eyes laughed up at him. Recognizing the flirtatious look on her friend's face, Brianna hastened to intervene. This knight, though young, looked to be more than even Mary could handle. His eyes roved boldly over the girl's figure, and even from this distance Brianna could see the flash of desire in his eyes.

"My lord is out patrolling the shire with some of his men," Brianna told him. "Was it he you wished to see?"

Without taking his eyes from Mary, the young man answered. "Aye. I bring a message from King William."

Irritated at Mary's refusal to recognize the danger to herself, Brianna rebuked her friend gently.

"Mary, think you not that it would be best for you to return to preparing the noontide meal?"

Mary's eyes met Brianna's and recognized the message flashing there. Shrugging, the young maid took herself into the keep with a last backward glance.

The knight now studied Brianna thoughtfully. Her dress was a fine velvet, her brown curls confined in a snood. Was she the mistress of this castle? Had Sir Garek married again? She hardly seemed his type. He could remember Garek's wife, her beauty and fire, and this lass had nothing like them to commend her.

"Pray, come inside for a refreshing drink," Brianna told him, turning to lead the way inside.

Dismounting, he handed his reins to a servant and followed the maid inside. It took a moment for his eyes to adjust to the darkness after the bright light of the sun.

"My lady, my name is Sir Hormis, late of Brittany. I would have a name to put to such a lovely lady as yourself."

Brianna smiled at the knight. "You have a smooth tongue, sir knight." As his face colored, Brianna's smile widened. "My name is Brianna."

"And are you. . .you are perhaps the lady of this manor?"

It had probably seemed so to the young man, the way she had appeared to order Mary around. He could not know of the friendship between the two and how, often, neither had to speak a word for the other to understand some message between them.

"Nay. I am but a servant here."

Looking immensely relieved, Sir Hormis followed Brianna to a table where she poured him a tankard of clear, cool water. Lifting it, he downed the contents without stopping. He handed the cup back to Brianna.

"Many thanks, Brianna."

She took the cup from him. "Please make yourself comfortable until my lord returns. If you will excuse me, I must needs attend to the noontide meal with Mary."

Sir Hormis's eyes followed Brianna as she crossed the room and entered the cooking chamber. He strained to see past her in hopes of gaining a glimpse of the bonny maid he had seen earlier. Disappointed, he settled back in his chair.

Mary handed Brianna a trencher of meat. "I know what you are about to say," Mary told her. "But do not berate me without just cause."

"Mary, you must needs be careful with these Norman knights. They have traveled far and have seen much. . .much hardship. They are looking for a little sport. I would not see you hurt."

Placing her hands on her hips, Mary smiled fondly at her friend. "I have known how to manage men from a young age. It is more likely you are the one who needs the warning. You leave the likes of these Normans to me."

"Mary!"

Ignoring her, Mary hefted the platter of bread and handed it to Brom, the pantler. "Blow the horn, Adam," she told the young man waiting beside her. Brianna kept any other comments to herself as she followed with the platter of meat.

Before long another shout heralded the return of Garek and his men. Having worried about him all morning, Brianna hastened to the door, waiting for Garek to dismount.

He strode past her and into the great room where the knights that had remained behind had gathered for their midday meal. He all but ignored Brianna. Seeing Sir Hormis, he stopped abruptly.

"What, ho, Hormis! A sight for sore eyes you are!"

Grinning, the young man rose and saluted his superior. "My liege, we have missed you sorely at King William's court."

They thumped each other on the back, laughing and jesting with each other. Only Brianna noticed that Garek favored his right arm.

"Milord," she asked softly. "You are injured?"

All eyes came to bear on the lord of the manor.

"It is nothing," he told her shortly. "Only a flesh wound."

"Shall I call for Alfred?"

"Nay," he told her roughly. "It is nothing, I say."

Hormis studied Garek speculatively. "You had a battle, Garek?"

Garek's eyes went swiftly to Brianna and away again. "Yea. We found the raiders that have been marauding our shire and those around us."

"Did you kill them?" the knight asked, and Brianna flinched at his eagerness.

"Aye."

Brianna's heart sank. She knew that in all probability Garek had had no choice, but still she wished there could be another way.

As Brianna and Mary served the meal, Garek watched in amusement as Hormis tried to maneuver Mary into agreeing to a tryst with him after dark. His eyes followed the maid wherever she went.

Garek's amusement fled when Brianna took Mary's place serving and the young knight continually tried to engage Brianna in conversation. He couldn't know that Hormis was earnestly entreating Brianna to speak a word in his favor to Mary.

Sir Bolson was less than pleased with the young knight also. As Mary flirted with Hormis, Bolson's mood grew darker.

"What brings you here?" Bolson asked the other knight.

Hormis's gaze reluctantly left Mary and turned to Bolson. "By my sword, I almost forgot. I have a message for you, Garek, from William."

The room grew quiet as all eyes turned to Hormis.

"William bids you come to London. You, and you alone. Your men are to remain here to protect the land. King William has aught he wishes to discuss with you. I have no knowledge of what he is about, I only know that it is something personal."

Brianna's heart sank. She saw Garek's face become a bland mask and she realized he would never let anyone know what he was thinking. He was so very good at hiding his true feelings.

"When am I to leave?"

"He wants you in London by the new year."

Garek studied his drinking horn as though it would give him some inkling of what was about to happen. What did William want from him now?

In a week it would be Christmas—one year since William's coronation. And a week later, another new year. What would the year 1068 bring? Garek had grown tired of warring and wished for nothing more than to stay in this shire and live at peace.

His eyes sought Brianna as she went about her duties. *What will happen to her in my absence?* He had a growing fondness for the wench and wished to see her protected. What was this feeling he had for the girl? It was not love. Nay, he had much experience of that in times past. He felt nothing like he had when he'd shared his life with various women. Nay, this was not love. Then what?

When she would have passed by him, Garek reached out a hand and took Brianna by the wrist. He tugged her gently until she fell across his lap.

Her eyes flew to his, questioning his motives. Garek stroked a hand up and down her arm as he turned to young Serin at his side. He struck up a conversation with the knight. When Brianna tried to rise, Garek kept her firmly in place.

Alarmed, Brianna tried unsuccessfully to gain Garek's attention. Realizing she could do nothing, she sat stiffly on his lap.

His stroking fingers were doing funny things to her insides and she wished herself anywhere but where she was. What was his game, anyway?

Mary entered the room, her eyes growing wide with surprise. Brianna threw her pleading looks, but there was nothing Mary could do.

Before long, Brianna noticed many eyes turned her way and her face grew red. Garek continued to ignore her as he laughed with his comrades.

Finally, Garek turned his attention back to Brianna. Her eyes were pleading for release but Garek was not finished yet.

Pulling her face down to his, Garek kissed her thoroughly before his watching men. Brianna pulled back from him, her heart thundering in her chest. She searched his face for some clue to his madness but could find none, while Garek smiled slowly into her astonished eyes. Finally, he released her.

Rising quickly, Brianna made her way rapidly from the room on legs that felt like jelly. Garek didn't watch her leave. His eyes were on his men. They looked from the fleeing Brianna to Garek and back again. Seeing the look in their eyes, Garek was satisfied. They would not bother the maid while he was gone. She would be safe from any unwanted attentions, for their fear of him was greater than their lust, and he had just marked the woman as his.

❧

Garek stood—fists on hips, feet braced apart—glaring at the girl before him. For the past three days she had avoided him totally. Now she faced him boldly, her anger unmistakable.

"Brianna, it is the only way!"

"Nay! I will not let you do it!"

Never had Garek seen Brianna in a temper. Her soft blue eyes turned to a deep sapphire, flashing in her anger. Her long brown curls were thrown back over her shoulder, and she gently clutched a tiny pup in her hands.

He had recently been adding hounds to the castle to be used for hunting, and one female came bearing a litter of pups.

The bright color in Brianna's cheeks and the angry sparkle in her eyes only enhanced her appearance, in Garek's way of thinking. Once again he tried to reason with her. "The pup cannot survive without his mother's milk. It is better that he die quickly than starve to death."

Tears came swiftly to her eyes. "There must be something we can do! How can a mother turn from her own blood?"

Garek reached for Brianna, intent on comforting her, but she hastily stepped away, thinking he meant to take the pup from her.

"Nay, I tell you!"

Brianna snuggled the small creature close against her bosom. She felt the pain of his rejection as though it were her own. Hadn't her own father disowned her in much the same way?

Brianna glared angrily at the mother dog, who was lying in the rushes oblivious of what was happening. The dog gently licked the pups that nuzzled her for their meal.

The dog had chosen this pup to die because she knew she could only feed a certain number, and hers was a large litter. Since this pup was the smallest and least likely to survive, she had pushed it away from her.

"Brianna."

She turned back to Garek. She faced him without fear, aware that he was fast losing patience with her.

"Give me the pup," he commanded, and his voice told her he meant to be obeyed.

Clutching the pup closer, she again shied away from him. "Nay! If you mean to harm this pup, then you must needs harm me first, for I will not give him over to you!"

It occurred to Garek that if the other women of England were like this stubborn, fiery vixen, England might well still be in English control.

It continued to amaze him that Brianna could be so passionate, never before losing her temper in his presence. He had no doubt that she meant what she said. There was no way he could part her from the pup without causing one of them some harm.

Turning, Brianna fled from the room into the kitchen, slamming the door behind her. Garek gazed at the door, a frown creasing his brow.

Sir Bolson stood at his side, an amused smirk on his face.

"What now, my liege?"

Garek barely glanced at him. "It is not my wont to hurt the maid, but neither can I let the poor beast suffer. The wench must listen to reason."

Pressing his lips tightly together, Garek followed after her. As he was about to open the door, Bolson grinned at him.

"Good luck, milord."

Garek quieted him with a look, opening the door into the cooking chamber.

He found Mary roasting a pig on a spit over the fire. She rapidly came to her feet.

"Milord?"

His eyes scanned the room. "Where is Brianna?"

"Brianna, milord? She took the back stairs to her room."

Garek went after her. He found himself outside a locked door.

"Brianna, open this door," he commanded.

When he heard no movement within, he banged loudly, shaking the portal with his anger. "Wench, open this door, or by heaven I will break it in!"

He could hear her slowly cross the room. She opened the door a crack and Garek saw her tear-ravaged face. Shoving the door wider, he strode into her room.

"Where is the pup?"

Brianna darted to the corner of the room where Garek could see a small wooden box. In it, Brianna had placed her old worn kirtle and gunna, wrapping the pup snugly inside.

Beside the box rested a flagon of milk and what had once been a falconer's glove. The smallest finger had been cut from the leather and set beside the bowl.

Forehead wrinkled, Garek turned to Brianna. "What are you about, woman?"

Without saying a word, Brianna dropped to her knees, taking the pup and carefully settling it on her lap. She crooned to the beast as she lifted the finger of the glove. Garek noticed a drop of milk dripping from a hole in the center of the finger.

Brianna adjusted the pup's head so that she could work the glove into its mouth. The pup tried to suck, grunting as its tiny mouth worked up and down.

Her head lowered over the creature, Brianna missed the long look Garek gave her. He felt something tightening in his chest as he stared at the bowed head beneath him. Her soft voice crooning to the pup did more than just soothe the beast.

Realizing he had not only lost the battle but the war as well, Garek left the room. Someday he would have to teach the wench about who ruled this great manor. He didn't realize that wagers were being made on who would teach whom.

## six

Christmastide came, and with it a celebration the likes of which the shire had never seen before, for the previous lord of the manor had been a miserly man with little concern for the welfare of his villeins.

Garek, on the other hand, showed himself to be generous and kind, though the people of the shire had found that his judgments were swift and sure.

Not a man, woman, or child would go hungry this year. Garek and his men provided the meat and the villeins added their own contributions. A huge feast in the manor brought on much merriment and revelry. The ale flowed freely, and Brianna worried as Garek's men became bolder in their advances toward the women. She herself had no worries, but Mary was having a hard time serving food and at the same time keeping her clothing where it belonged. So were many of the other serving maids.

Brianna wished the night a speedy end, for she knew in the morning the men would be as tame as kittens, especially with their pounding headaches. Much of their play was harmless, but well she knew the effects of drink, having a brother who freely imbibed.

Garek's attention was on other things. A small smile played about his lips as he watched Bolson and Hormis vie for Mary's attention. He turned and caught Brianna staring at him. His eyes met hers and Brianna found herself unable to look away. *What is he thinking that causes his eyes to darken to the color of a stormy sea?* she wondered.

A sudden clatter took their attention. Mary stood arms akimbo, glaring at the two knights seated before her. Flashing eyes warned Brianna that her friend was in a fine temper. Taking a drink from the table, Mary dumped it on each knight in turn.

"Perhaps that will cool you off," she told them angrily before turning and striding from the room.

Amid guffaws from the men present, Brianna rose to follow her friend, but Garek took her by the wrist.

"I have meant to ask you about the pup."

It had been two days and still the pup was alive. To Brianna's eyes it appeared to be growing, although she supposed that was wishful thinking. She had no doubt that if Garek thought otherwise, the pup would meet a speedy end, for Garek hated to see anything suffer.

"He is well, milord."

His eyes studied hers, and giving a brief nod, he released her. "It is good," he told her.

Brianna marveled that such a large, fearsome knight could be as gentle and caring as this one was. It was hard to believe that he would really have harmed such a small creature as the pup. At the same time, she found that his anger could flame to life with the least provocation, though to be honest, there was usually justification.

She recalled those thoughts the next morning when she stood on the castle steps watching proceedings in the courtyard.

A man bowed before Garek, his head hung over his bent knee awaiting the sentence he thought was surely to come. Brianna recognized him as one of Garek's knights, though the man had found no favor in her eyes. There was something about him that Brianna didn't trust. She had encountered men like him before and had reason to dislike them.

Garek was talking to the man in such quiet tones that Brianna hadn't a chance of hearing what was being said, but from the color of the other man's face, it couldn't have been good.

A young girl stood at Garek's side, her face lowered in

shame. Brianna recognized the lass as the youngest daughter of the old woman who produced fine stitchery in the village. The girl's name was Aleene, and she was as sweet as her mother was cruel.

As the lord continued to speak, the girl's face took on a frightened cast, her large blue eyes pleading for a mercy Brianna couldn't understand.

When Garek finished speaking to the man, the man looked up at Garek, then at Aleene, then back to Garek. Slowly he nodded his head.

Aleene threw herself at Garek's feet, and even from this distance Brianna had no trouble hearing her beg for mercy.

Garek's eyes swiftly roamed the circle of faces surrounding him, at last fastening upon Brianna. Motioning her to his side, Brianna made her way down the steps of the keep and across the courtyard.

If not for the seriousness of the situation, Brianna would have laughed at the harassed expression on Garek's face.

"My lord?"

"Take the wench inside and see if you can calm her," he told Brianna, motioning to the girl still kneeling in the dirt at his feet.

Brianna helped Aleene to her feet, murmuring soothing words. Brianna had no idea what had transpired, but the girl looked frightened to death.

Seating the girl on a bench in the great room, Brianna knelt before her, placing her hands gently on the girl's, which were twisted together in her lap.

"Aleene," she murmured softly. "Tell me what has happened."

Tears were coursing in floods down the other girl's cheeks as her eyes found Brianna's. Seeing the sympathy there, Aleene buried her face in her hands and began rocking back and forth, moaning.

"Oh, Brianna, I would rather die!"

"Shh, Aleene. You would rather die than what? What has happened?"

Brianna pulled the girl's hands from her face. Curling her fingers around Aleene's shoulders, she shook her slightly.

"Tell me!"

The girl stared helplessly into Brianna's eyes before bursting into tears again. Flustered, Brianna turned when Garek walked into the room, his look settling on Aleene.

"Falstaff has agreed to marry you," he told the girl, his voice harsher than he intended.

Brianna rose to her feet in surprise. "Marry her? Falstaff?"

Garek looked as though he would rather be anywhere than that place. He had never been able to deal with a woman's tears, and this was no exception. He shrugged helplessly.

"The girl was deflowered. There must needs be restitution. Her mother demands it."

Whirling, Brianna dropped to the girl's side again. "Oh, Aleene. I did not know. How awful for you!"

Aleene turned pleading eyes to Garek. "I beg you, milord. Don't make me marry the man!"

"What say you, woman? Your mother has demanded it, and Falstaff swore an oath to protect such as you. He chose to break that vow; now he can face the consequences."

"But she does not love Falstaff!" Brianna argued.

Garek's face flooded with color. "It is not of love I speak. Falstaff has wrongly used the wench, and he must make amends. Would you condemn the girl to a lonely life without any man to care for her?"

For the second time in only a few days, Brianna's face was animated by her anger. Her eyes flashed fire. "Falstaff violated her and you would give her over to the man?"

"What else would you have me do? Her mother insists on it, I tell you."

"Her mother be hanged!"

Garek's eyebrows flew up at this unaccustomed outburst.

He had never heard the girl speak a wrong word about anyone.

"Garek," she pleaded. "There is more to this than you understand."

Crossing his arms over his chest, he stared at Brianna belligerently. "Then make me understand."

Aleene looked from one to the other. Her hope was pinned on Brianna, but the giant knight looked as unmovable as a stone statue.

"It is not a husband Aleene's mother seeks for her but a means of support. She knows that your knights are from wealthy families. She has never cared what happened to Aleene, and as you can see, she doesn't care now, either. She is only looking for money."

He looked from her to Aleene, sighing. "Perhaps what you say is true, but the girl has been deflowered and has no hope of finding a husband now."

Aleene hung her head, but Brianna wouldn't give up. "Ask."

"What?"

"Ask if there are any who would consider Aleene for a wife."

Garek stared at her as though she had suddenly lost her mind. "Who would you have me ask?"

Brianna flung her hand towards the castle door. "Ask your knights. Ask the villagers."

They faced each other a long time before Garek took Aleene by the arm and, muttering to himself, he strode across the hall. Slamming open the door, he exited the hall.

Brianna followed at his heels, not sure she had done the right thing. Still, Brianna had watched the growing relationship between Serin and young Aleene, and she hoped the young knight would come to the girl's aid now. It was obvious to everyone that they had feelings for each other. The question was, how strong were those feelings?

Garek stood at the top of the stairs, facing the crowd below that awaited his decision. He lifted Aleene's hand in the air, and when he spoke, his deep voice was heard even to the far-thest reaches of the crowd.

"This girl has no wish to marry Sir Falstaff, nor he her. Is there any man here that would be willing to take his place? Otherwise, the marriage will occur as I have said."

Shivering with the cold, Brianna searched the crowd for Serin's face. When she couldn't find him, her heart began to pound. Where could he be?

Garek was aggravated at having to be put in this position. His face burned with embarrassment, both for himself and the girl standing silently at his side. He glared angrily at Brianna.

The crowd grew ominously quiet. No sounds could be heard save the rustling of clothing as each person looked at those around them.

"I will marry the girl."

Brianna sighed with relief. Serin pushed his way forward, coming to stand at the bottom of the steps. His dark eyes were fastened upon Aleene.

Surprised, Garek looked from one to the other. "What say you, maid? Is Sir Serin acceptable to you as a husband?"

Aleene nodded her head, her eyes shining. "Aye, milord."

Not altogether sure of what was happening, but relieved nonetheless, Garek motioned for the young knight to take the girl's hand.

Even Aleene's mother was satisfied, for it mattered not to her which knight her daughter married, so long as he had wealth. And since Serin was sheriff as well as knight, she was more than content to share her daughter's good fortune.

Brianna smiled happily at the young couple, her face bright with her pleasure. Garek was pleased to have caused her such joy, though he was still not sure what had just taken place.

He was still mulling it over in his mind that evening when he called Bolson to him, giving over charge of the fief in his absence. Bolson seemed more than relieved that Sir Hormis was returning to London with Garek.

Garek found himself reluctant to go. In spite of what he had said earlier, he seemed to have planted roots in this English countryside. Here he had found the peace that had eluded him for so long. Even the dreams were no longer as frequent as before.

Brianna entered from the kitchen, stopping abruptly when she realized that Sir Bolson was with Garek. Bolson turned from his contemplations of the view outside the window, as Garek motioned her into the chamber.

"Milord, I have repaired your tunic," she told Garek, handing him the garment.

"My thanks, Brianna. I feared it beyond saving and it was a favorite of mine."

Bolson excused himself and left the room. Brianna was about to do the same when Garek halted her.

"Stay," he commanded softly.

Uncertain of his mood, she moved across the room and gingerly sat upon a stool close to the hearth. Remembering the last time she had sat here with Garek, Brianna felt hot color come to her cheeks.

"You wished to speak with me?"

Garek turned from her and began packing the supplies he would need for his trip, placing them in a sack. He frowned. Why had he asked the girl to stay?

"How soon will you leave?" Brianna asked.

"Before first light tomorrow."

Brianna fell silent. Her reluctance to see Garek leave was unsettling, for it hinted at feelings she was loathe to acknowledge. Would she ever see him again? The thought of not doing so sent a strange pain lancing through her heart.

"I wish you Godspeed," she told him quietly.

He stopped what he was doing, turning to face her. He studied her bent head, but there was nothing about her that gave away any of her thoughts or feelings. He would miss her sorely, for her gentleness and compassion were rare among the women of his acquaintance.

"If you have any needs, you are to take them to Sir Bolson, do you understand?"

"Yea, milord."

He came to her side, kneeling before her. "You are not to hesitate," he stressed.

She looked into his eyes, her own unsure. What did he want from her? What exactly was he trying to say?

Garek took her small hand in his larger one, studying it as though it would have the answers to all his questions.

"Is there aught you wish from London?"

She shook her head and his eyes returned to her face. "Nay, there is nothing."

Taking her hand from his, Brianna rose to leave. "I have work to do, milord. If there is nothing else. . ."

Rising to his feet also, Garek looked down at her. There was nothing to keep her here but he found himself unwilling to let her go. It suddenly occurred to him that he might never see her again, for there was no telling what King William had in store for him.

Cupping her face in the palms of his hands, he told her huskily, "Nothing, save this."

When his lips came down on hers, Brianna felt her heart leap within her breast. Closing her eyes, she savored the pleasure of the moment.

The kiss ended long before Brianna wanted it to, and her eyes fluttered open, their color intensified by the unexpected desire she had felt. *For the first time in my life I understand what a temptation love can bring.*

There. She had admitted it to herself. She loved Garek. At least she supposed that what she felt was love, although she had no way of knowing. Her lack of experience left her vulnerable.

Garek watched the emotions flitting across her face, and for the first time in his life he thought of someone else before himself.

"Go to bed, Brianna," he told her, his voice still soft with his own desire.

Nodding, she turned and left him standing there. When she reached the door, she looked back and found him still watching her. She went out, closing the door softly behind her.

❧

Garek mounted his horse, adjusting himself to the saddle. Briefly his gaze focused on Brianna standing in the doorway of the keep, light from the torches spilling out from behind her. Her face in shadow, he had no way of knowing what she might be thinking.

Sir Hormis tightened the girth on his own saddle before himself climbing on. He grinned at Garek, his eyes bright with enthusiasm for the trip to come.

"Shall we?"

Garek didn't return his smile. He nodded his head once before turning his steed down the road.

Brianna watched until the darkness swallowed them, shivering on the threshold. Finally, Mary called her inside.

Climbing the stairs to her bed chamber, Brianna went first to her knees to petition the Lord on Garek's behalf, then she went to the box beside the fire where the puppy lay sleeping.

She smiled as she listened to its little grunts. She hadn't as yet named him, and decided perhaps that would be an appropriate name: Grunt.

Laughing, she reached down to stroke the dog. "Nay," she told it softly. "You must needs have a regal name to make up for your shortcomings in life."

The puppy woke and began nuzzling her hand. Lifting him from the box, Brianna took up the makeshift feeder and let him have his way with it. Milk drizzled down the sides of its mouth and onto her gunna.

"Garek would call you merely 'hound,' but we know you are something special, do we not?"

The pup continued to feed greedily at the glove finger,

heedless of all else, while Brianna pondered a name for him.

"I know. I shall call you Loup. Perhaps you will live up to your name and be a bold and cunning hunter."

It never occurred to her that she had chosen the French version of the word. What would Garek think of her naming the dog after the wolves that roamed the countryside? Perhaps he would never know. She again felt a pang at the thought that she might never see him again. What would happen to her then? Already she missed him unbearably, and he had only been gone moments.

Days turned into weeks and still there was no word from Garek. Even Bolson began to fret at his delay in returning.

"I was not meant to be lord of an English manor," he told Brianna. "If anything, I would prefer my home in Normandy."

Brianna smiled as she laid a platter of meat before him. "Do you dislike us then so much, Sir Bolson?"

His eyes went past her to Mary, who was serving the other men. "Nay. It is not the English I dislike, though there are some I could easily lay a sword to."

Brianna followed his look. Mary was laughing with a young man who had been conscripted to help Gaylan in the castle. His ruddy good looks and cheerful disposition had made him a favorite with both Brianna and Mary. The boy was eager to work and anxious to please.

If one could call him a boy. At a score plus four he was a man, but to Brianna he still seemed a youth, though he was but two years younger than she—and the same age as Mary.

Grinning, Brianna left the trencher on the table before Sir Bolson and returned to the kitchen. She opened the door that led outside to a back courtyard and descended the steps to where a small herb garden was located.

Walking along the path, she stared up at the stars. A fortnight had come and gone, and still no word from Garek. Was he all right? Had William perhaps sent him off to battle some other enemy now that the English had been subdued?

Pulling her shawl tightly about her, she sat down on a large stone. She sucked in her breath as the cold of the rock penetrated her clothes.

Instead of returning to the warmth of the keep, she moved so that the breeze blowing from the north no longer hit her full force. She needed time to think, and this was the best place to do it.

Lifting her eyes to the sky, she once again entreated the Lord on Garek's behalf.

"Wherever he is, Lord, keep him safe."

❧

Garek studied the same stars that night, in London. He missed Brianna more than he ever thought it was possible to miss anyone. He missed her soothing presence, her soft laugh, her gentle teasing. She was on his mind constantly. Especially since the dreams had returned.

The balcony door opened behind him and King William walked out.

"There you are, Garek. I have been looking for you."

Bowing low, Garek gave the man his attention. "I am sorry, Sire. I did not know."

"Come back inside, man; you will freeze to death out here."

Garek followed his king back inside. What was it William wanted from him? It had been over a fortnight and still he had no idea why he had been summoned.

He followed the king across the lavishly decorated ballroom to the dais at the end. William seemed to be waiting for something, his eyes continually going to the room's entrance.

"Have a seat, Garek," he told his knight, indicating the table to his right. "I have a surprise for you."

The sounds in the room jangled Garek's nerves. He hated crowds, royal ones or not. He longed for the peace and quiet of his own hall.

Smiling wryly, he shook his head slightly. How was it that he had changed so much in just the last few months? Several women had tried to strike up a conversation with him, but even the most beautiful had stirred only a passing interest in him. Instead, he continually saw huge, innocent blue eyes in his mind.

A trumpeting fanfare brought the room to instant stillness.

"His lord, the Earl of Waverly, and his lovely daughter Marie," the herald intoned regally.

Garek noticed the smile that lit William's face when the man was announced. Earl Waverly made his way to the king's throne, bowing low. His daughter dropped into a curtsy, her beguiling smile charming the king into returning it.

They began an animated conversation that held no interest for Garek. He lifted his cup and began to study the people around him.

When a shadow fell over him, he lifted his eyes to encounter William's smiling face.

"Garek, come with us. We have something to discuss with you."

The "us" in question seemed to include the earl and his young daughter.

Rising to his feet, Garek followed them from the ballroom to the king's counsel chambers. The king motioned for them to be seated.

"Garek, my friend, I have talked with my oldest and dearest friend, Earl Waverly, and he has agreed. . ."

Garek frowned in confusion. "Sire?"

William laughed. "I am sorry, Garek, you have no idea of the plans we have been hatching, have you?"

Garek looked from one man to the other. William was pleased with whatever plan he had devised, but the earl's look could only be described as smug.

And the girl? What had she to do with anything? She looked perfectly content, her beautiful face devoid of any emotion.

William continued. "The earl has agreed to allow you to marry his daughter."

## seven

Garek paced up and down in the antechamber, slamming his fist into his palm. Never in his wildest imaginings could he have expected this from William.

There was something in William's voice that convinced Garek that this was no request. Obviously, there was a purpose behind this marriage proposal, but he had yet to find out what it was.

He glared around him at the rich surroundings. Gritting his teeth, he jerked a beautiful brocade tapestry from the wall where it hung, flinging it to the floor. Perhaps that was not wise, but it had given him immeasurable satisfaction.

What excuse had he given William before he fled the room? He couldn't remember, but he knew William would expect him to return, and in a timely manner. It would not do to offend the earl and his beautiful daughter.

Taking a deep breath, he tried to calm himself. He must have his wits about him, and his anger did little toward achieving that goal. If he wanted to know the king's reasoning, then he had better return to the king's counsel chambers. He could always say no.

Garek laughed without mirth. Indeed he could say no, offending the earl, losing favor with the king, and in all likelihood winding up a pauper with no country to speak of. Either that or lose his head.

He knew his reasoning must be faulty, for William was a rational man not prone to imprudent decisions. Which brought his thoughts full circle to the objective for this marriage.

Swallowing his rage and frustration, Garek returned to the king and his companions.

The earl was studying him through narrowed eyes, probably wondering if the king had chosen rightly.

As for William, he continued much as though the conversation had never ceased.

"Jonathan has been a good friend to me, Garek. Loyal beyond most, even though that loyalty cost him his lands in England."

Garek waited for him to continue, his look settling on the earl's daughter. What was her name? Ah, yes, Marie. She sat with lowered lashes, a picture of genteel innocence. Garek wondered just how innocent she was in the scheme of things.

"Jonathan's lands were given by Harold to another English lord, therefore he has no more lands to call his own," William continued. "His daughter's marriage to you would serve two purposes. One, he would be assured that his children and grandchildren would have their rightful inheritance. Second, he would have the protection of one of my finest knights, as well as a bond between one of France's finest families and one of England's."

William certainly was logical. Garek couldn't fault his reasoning. Many a knight would jump at the chance, and it was true the damsel was fair to look upon. Rarely had he seen such a beautiful woman.

When she looked up at him, her green eyes were vacant, and Garek knew she was hiding her own feelings in the matter. Such women made him uncomfortable. He much preferred Brianna's open honesty.

He couldn't tell her hair color, it being hidden beneath her cloth wimple, but her lashes were a dark auburn, highlighting her creamy white complexion.

When she dropped her lashes, Garek turned back to the king. "Am I then to suppose that the lands your majesty has deeded to me are those belonging to Earl Waverly?"

"Nay, Garek," William answered. "Jonathan's lands were deeded to some of the barons and earls of Harold's choice.

Those lands I cannot give back to him for they were part of the agreement made with these men to lay down their arms."

"I see."

Indeed he did. He understood William's reasoning, but why had he chosen Garek? Other knights had families just as noble, if not more so.

"Yours is not the only marriage being arranged, Garek. I need trusted men in strategic places. For the security of France. For the security of England. Do you understand?"

Garek understood. This was a royal command, not a choice. He owed William his allegiance. He had sworn it to him. But did this include a choice of a life mate? He had no desire to marry again. He would never put his trust in another woman. But such a marriage as William proposed held no such concern for him, for he didn't love the woman in question.

And what of the girl herself? Had she any thoughts on the matter? He would like to know, but he knew her father would make that impossible. At least for now.

"I understand, Sire."

William's face was wreathed in smiles. "Good. I knew that you would not let me down, Garek."

The rest of the evening passed in a fog for Garek, his thoughts in turmoil. He excused himself from the festivities as soon as possible and found his way to his bed chamber.

The dream returned that night and the darkness was even more intense than before. This time Marie Waverly stood in his way as he tried to reach the light. He couldn't get around her, and as he watched, the light grew farther and farther away until he was at last left in total inky blackness.

&

Three months after he had left, word came that Garek was on his way and would reach them by nightfall. Brianna hurried to set things to right and make sure a hot meal would be awaiting him.

She couldn't deny the excitement she felt at the prospect of seeing him again, but she also was fearful of what his thoughts were concerning her, since he had been away so long.

He had been kind to her, but she had to admit that, except for that one tender kiss, he had shown her little that could be construed as romantic interest. If anything, he had been indifferent at best.

Bolson found her in the kitchen as she was about to mix batter for the bread.

"Garek has sent word to prepare two bed chambers for guests who will be arriving with him this eventide."

"Guests?" Hastily Brianna dropped the bowl on the table, untying the rag from around her waist.

"I know not who these guests are," Bolson told her, "but they will be staying for quite some time."

Brianna hurried from the kitchen. Calling two of the serving maids, she made haste to prepare two of the better rooms on the third floor that were as yet unoccupied.

It had been a long time since this manor had experienced such excitement. Brianna felt excitement as she found fresh bedding for the rooms. Was it the thought of guests, or was her happiness due to the lord's return?

Mary was in the kitchen, already preparing a feast, when Brianna came back.

"So, his lordship returns. Perhaps that is the cause for the sparkle in your eyes," Mary jested, throwing Brianna a teasing glance.

"In that case, the gleam in your own eyes must needs be from knowing that Sir Hormis has returned with him."

Surprised, Mary whirled on Brianna. "In truth?"

"Yea, you did not know?"

"Nay," she answered slowly, the gleam in her eyes growing brighter with her own thoughts. "But it is good news nonetheless."

Brianna began to lay the platters with cheese and meat. It

concerned her that Mary played so lightly with Sir Bolson's affections, for it was obvious that the knight was taken with her. He would make a fine husband for Mary, though there was no telling where the man's thoughts lay on that issue.

Everything was ready when the watchman finally called from the tower. Dusk was just settling over the countryside, and the temperature was beginning to drop, though they were far from the icy cold of winter.

Instead of a few riders, Garek was at the head of a long retinue. Brianna's heart gave a leap when she spotted him head and shoulders above everyone.

She searched his face and found it held no hint of his thoughts.

At his side was a tall man, his dark hair streaked with gray. Though he wore it long in the manor of the English, his face was clean shaven. He was a handsome man and would be handsomer still if he would smile, Brianna thought.

Behind him, a beautiful woman sat perched atop a lovely black mare. Unconsciously, Brianna's mouth dropped open, her eyes wide. Never had she seen such a beautiful woman. Her features were perfect, and there was no smile upon her fair face.

Another woman followed this one, and Brianna assumed she must be the fair woman's guardian, or nurse, for she was much older than the other.

In the hubbub of activity surrounding her, Brianna found Garek's eyes watching her. He hastily turned away, going to the young woman and helping her from her steed.

Brianna felt a twinge of jealousy as the woman laid her hand possessively on Garek's arm. What was this woman to Garek? Had he perchance found himself another wife while in London? Perhaps he had finally laid to rest the dark demons of his past. If so, she would be glad for him, though her heart felt as though it were breaking.

She shook away such thoughts. Here she was imagining the

worst, and she had yet to meet the lady.

Refusing to meet Brianna's look, Garek led the procession into the great hall and bid them find seats near the fire.

Although Garek had avoided Brianna, he was aware of her with every fiber of his being. He had wondered how he would feel after seeing Brianna again—now he knew. His heart had raced at the sight of her and he had found it hard to keep his thoughts in check. Her soft blue eyes were everything he remembered. Innocent. Untouched. Gentle. And though she was probably unaware, glowing with love.

Sir Hormis made his presence known immediately. His laughter did much to dispel the gloom that seemed to have fallen over the castle. Instead of rejoicing, there seemed to be an anxious expectation that something disagreeable were about to happen.

Mary bustled about with serving platters, as did Brianna and several others. Garek rose to his feet, lifting a horn of ale into the air.

"A toast," he boomed, and sudden quiet descended. Garek's gaze roamed the hall, resting momentarily on Brianna. He turned back to the man at his side. "To my future father and my future bride."

If the room was quiet before, not a sound could be heard now.

Brianna's heart wrenched at the announcement, although she had expected something of the sort. Somehow, she had known it all along.

Abruptly the room broke into cheers, and Brianna saw Garek fall back into his seat. She knew he was watching her, but she resisted looking his way again.

Garek's men surged as one to Garek's side, thumping him on the back and offering congratulations. The room grew loud with their revelry.

When the opportunity presented itself, Brianna left the hall and returned to the kitchen. Taking a wrap from behind the door, she called to Loup, who hastily rose from his place by the kitchen fire.

Brianna exited the kitchen by the back stairs and found her favorite spot in the garden. She dropped to her knees, hugging Loup tightly. Her tears wet his fur, and the pup pulled back from her, struggling against her tight grip.

Reaching up, Loup began to lick the tears from her face, his soft whine telling of his confusion at these strange proceedings.

Brianna let him go, getting to her feet and making her way to the bench that overlooked the marshes at the rear of the castle. How long she sat thus she didn't know, but the sudden creaking of the kitchen door brought her head around.

She wasn't surprised to see Garek standing there, though he made no move to come to her. With the light spilling out from behind him, Brianna could barely make out his features. His wary gaze wandered over her face, noting the tracks from her tears.

Brushing away the remnants, Brianna tried to smile. She managed a faltering twist of the lips. "I am pleased to see you well, milord."

"And I you," he returned softly. He started to descend the stairs when he was brought up short by a low growl. Surprised, he turned to find himself being eyed by the young pup, his ears pinned close to his head and his chest heaving with his puppy growl.

Brianna went and lifted him into her arms, cuddling him close. "Shhh, Loup. Sir Garek is a friend."

"Is this the pup you rescued from death?"

"Yea. As you can see, he is alive and well."

Garek shook his head slowly. "I would never have believed it. The beast is a monstrous size!"

His eyes found Brianna's and they were alight with humor. "It would seem he has become your protector."

Brianna didn't smile. "Do I need protecting, milord?"

The laughter fled from his eyes. "Nay, Brianna. I only came

to see if you are well. I. . ."

He stopped. What could he say?

"She is very beautiful," Brianna told him.

He took a long time answering. "Aye."

Garek realized there was nothing more to be said, but he was loath to leave without some explanation, though why he should have to explain to a servant was unclear to him. He only knew that Brianna was hurt, and he wanted to comfort her.

Brianna, in turn, studied Garek's face. He looked tired, though he was as handsome as ever. There was no happiness in his visage as should have befitted an engaged man. She wondered what the story was behind this marriage.

Garek came and stood before her and Loup's growling increased. Brianna clung to the dog as though her life depended on it.

"Brianna, I am sorry if I have hurt you."

She could tell he meant it. Had he surmised her feelings? She knew her open face was often her worse enemy. Burying her face in the pup's fur, she tried to get her thoughts together.

Finally, she looked up at him, her eyes clear. "I will get over it, milord. A foolish girl's infatuation with a handsome man, no more. It will soon pass."

Garek frowned, not liking what she had to say. "Brianna. . ."

She whirled, retreating farther into the shadows. She still cuddled the pup, who was watching Garek with a leery eye.

"If that is all, milord, I must prepare for bed. Tomorrow will be a busy day."

Garek watched her a long time before he turned abruptly on his heels and left, leaving the kitchen door open behind him.

Releasing her breath slowly, Brianna dropped the puppy to the ground. Rubbing her throbbing temples with her fingers, she tried to decide what to do.

She couldn't stay here, but neither could she leave. It was forbidden for villeins to leave the manor without the lord's permission. Would Garek give her that permission?

Slowly she returned to the keep, but instead of going to the great hall, she climbed the back stairs to her room.

Taking off her gunna, she folded it neatly and lay it on the chest at the foot of her bed. She climbed under the furs, her teeth chattering with cold.

Loup jumped up on the bed beside her, curling against her legs. She welcomed his warmth, though in the summer she would probably regret that she had allowed him to sleep on her bed.

Soon the warmth and her own tired thoughts lulled her into a restless sleep.

❧

Bolson glared at the man before him. "I want no part of your crazy shenanigans! Keep your land!"

Garek stared at his friend in astonishment. "What ails you, man? You did not feel this way before when I offered to make you a vassal of my fief."

Bolson was at a loss to explain his feelings. He only knew that this big oaf standing before him had hurt Brianna, and it angered him beyond reason. Well he could remember times when the gentle maid had talked with him about his feelings and thoughts, especially regarding Mary. She was kind to a fault, inspiring his own urge to protect her.

"And what of the wench?"

Confused, Garek studied his friend through narrowed eyes. "What wench?"

"Brianna. What of her?"

"What of her?" The ominous tone of Garek's voice should have warned the young knight, but he was past heeding.

"She is not like others, Garek. She is kind and sensitive. She should not be hurt."

"And what would you have me do?" he asked softly.

Bolson threw his hands in the air. "Do? It is beyond my ken, but you must do something!"

"Perhaps you have feelings for the wench?"

Something in Garek's voice finally got through to Bolson. His eyes went wide at the look on Garek's face and he swallowed hard.

"Nay, Garek. It is only that the girl has been kind to me. I hate to see her hurt."

Garek relaxed slightly, though his anger was far from spent. "You are getting soft in your old age, my friend. It is not like you to be so concerned with a woman's feelings."

"This one is different," he insisted, and Garek felt his anger rise again.

"If you do not wish to have a manor on this fief, then what do you wish?"

Bolson turned from him, studying the kitchen door. "Of late I have been thinking of returning to Normandy."

Garek was so surprised, he could only stare. What would he do without his best friend and longtime confidante? Things were happening too quickly. He felt himself out of control, unable to command events happening around him.

"Etienne, this makes no sense."

"Aye, Garek. Nothing seems to make sense anymore." He turned to his friend and ventured the question others were too afraid to ask.

"What did William offer you in exchange for this marriage?"

If not for their longtime friendship, Garek would have knocked Bolson into the rushes.

"Things are not always what they seem," Garek told him quietly. "But if I were you, I would not venture forth to London at this particular time or you might find yourself in a similar position."

Bolson sighed. "I am sorry, Garek. Perhaps I am envious. My mind grows weary of warring and never having a place to call home."

"Then make your home here. Put down roots and raise a family."

"Is that what you plan to do? With Marie Waverly?"

Garek's mind rebelled at the thought.

"You do not answer. It is as I thought," he told Garek smugly.

"Tell me your thoughts," Garek commanded, his voice like soft velvet.

"It is not a green-eyed vixen that has won your heart, Garek, but a blue-eyed angel."

Eyes flashing fire, Garek scowled at his friend. "You missed your calling, my friend. You should be a wandering minstrel singing songs of love and spouting foolish poetry."

Mary entered the room, stopping short on seeing the two men in the hall so late in the day. "Pardon, my lord." She exited as rapidly as she had entered.

Garek smiled wryly. "Perhaps you should turn your prose upon another."

Bolson's eyes grew cold. "I am a man, not a boy. I gave up childish games long ago and have no desire to embark upon them again. Perhaps Sir Hormis finds them more to his liking."

With that, the young knight left the room, leaving Garek staring dumbfounded after him.

That evening, Brianna found herself serving the soon-to-be lady of the manor. The girl's brilliant green eyes held a sadness in their depths that Brianna found herself responding to.

Marie said very little, trying to make herself as inconspicuous as possible, but her beauty alone would not permit it. Many eyes wandered her way through the evening. Earl Waverly watched proceedings in the great hall without appearing to do so. As yet, no one could decide whether or not the two would be a welcome addition.

Mary let her feelings be known in no uncertain terms. At first, Brianna was afraid it was due to jealousy over Marie's beauty, but she soon came to realize that Mary considered the earl a traitor to his country, and no doubt there were others who would feel the same.

Since the earl had sided with William, many Englishmen

would not take kindly to his presence. Brianna feared there would be trouble, although she knew the manor was well protected.

Brianna watched Garek when he was around the girl, and though he treated her with the utmost courtesy, he showed none of the signs of being in love.

At the same time, Mary seemed to take great pleasure in flirting with Sir Hormis. At every opportunity she made it known that she found him more than interesting.

In turn, Sir Bolson developed a liking for Brianna's company. He would quickly come to her side when he thought she needed help, laughing at her teasing and playing the part of suitor.

Two pairs of eyes followed their play. Garek felt rage begin to churn inside him. Hadn't the girl said she felt a mere infatuation and that she would soon be over it? Well, it seemed she had. He began to doubt Bolson's claim that there was nothing between them.

Mary, on the other hand, had no idea what Bolson was about. She grew irritable with Brianna and chided her on any and every occasion. Though Brianna suspected the young knight's motives, she kept her thoughts to herself. Bolson's play provided Brianna with the opportunity to let Garek know that he need not concern himself with her.

In time, Brianna's gentle answers to Mary's barbs soon had the other girl begging pardon for her treatment of Brianna.

All in all, it was a turbulent time for Brianna and, she suspected, for others as well.

Lying awake in her chamber several nights later, Brianna heard loud voices in the courtyard outside. Crossing quickly to the window, she could barely make out the shapes of two men, one smaller than the other. The larger of the two was easily recognizable. Garek was in a fine temper, and though his rage flowed all around the smaller man, still the smaller held his ground.

When he stepped into the moonlight, Brianna could make out Bolson's fine features, and he seemed in as great a rage as the man he was arguing with.

The two stood thus for several minutes before Bolson turned quickly on his heel and strode away. Garek stood staring after him, his hands clenching and unclenching at his sides. His glance came up to Brianna's window and she hastily moved back out of sight, although she doubted he could see her from this distance.

In the morning, Sir Bolson was gone.

## eight

The next several days were trying for Brianna. Mary moped around the keep, ill of temper. She began to ruin the food she was preparing, and those around her began to grumble.

Garek nearly drove his men and his servants to distraction. Relentlessly he pushed his men—sword practice, jousting, hand-to-hand combat—until Brianna thought they would revolt.

During this stormy time Brianna came to know Marie Waverly better, for it was her duty to help the maid while she was at the keep. At first the young girl seemed sullen and remote, but Brianna soon found that was Marie's way of disguising her true feelings.

Marie was in awe of Garek. It didn't take Brianna long to discover that Marie lived in fear of the day she would become mistress of his manor. Lately, with Garek perpetually in a fit of anger, the girl positively quaked when he entered the room.

Earl Waverly seemed to watch Garek closely, and it was easy to see he worried that he might not have chosen wisely for his only child.

Brianna had decided that whatever the circumstances, Garek had made a vow to this girl, and she would do all in her power to see things made right. She loved Garek, true, but hers was an unselfish love. She would rather see him happy than watch him make himself, and those around him, miserable.

To this end she tried to get to know Marie and better help her understand the man who would one day become her husband. She knew Garek sometimes raged, but she also knew that he could be kindness itself.

What had provoked this current attitude of his was not of her understanding. She feared it had something to do with Sir

Bolson, but she didn't know what to do about it.

Each day, Brianna took Loup for a walk along the marsh paths, sometimes with Marie, other times not, and this day was no exception. Breathing in deeply of the rich air, Brianna felt the exhilaration of the season. Spring had burst forth in all its glory, the wildflowers peeking through the dark soil.

The warmth of the sun encouraged her to go farther than she had before, Loup trotting contentedly at her side. From time to time the pup would rush ahead to investigate something only he could sense, and then he would quickly return to her side.

Grinning at his playfulness, Brianna almost tripped over the man lying in her path. Pulling back in fright, she stared in horror at the motionless figure before her.

Loup was instantly at her side, his ears cocked forward as he investigated the inert figure. At his prodding, the man moaned, rolling to his back. Brianna gasped as she recognized the young stable lad who had ridden out only that morning with Sir Hormis and Earl Waverly.

She quickly knelt beside him, searching for signs of injury. As her hand passed over his back, it came away red with the boy's blood.

Knowing it was futile for her to try to move the lad, Brianna decided to go for help. She only hoped she would be in time. She hated to leave him there, but she had no other choice.

Lifting her gunna, she ripped a piece from her garment beneath, placing it against the wound on the boy's back. She tied it in place tightly, hoping it would stem the flow of blood.

Getting quickly to her feet, she commanded Loup to stay. She turned and ran toward the keep. She was out of breath by the time she reached the courtyard.

Already Garek's men were rushing to her side, having been warned by the watchman. Garek came striding out of the keep, quickly descending the stone steps, and Brianna collapsed in his arms.

"Brianna?"

The blood on her gunna drained Garek's face of color. He lifted her in his arms and was about to carry her inside when Brianna began to struggle.

"Nay, not me, Garek." Her breathing came torn and ragged and she had a hard time making herself clear. "Put me down."

He stopped in his tracks but refused to release her.

"You are hurt!"

"Nay, I tell you. In the marsh. . .it is the lad George."

Garek slowly returned her to her feet, his arm still holding her close.

"What say you?"

Brianna pushed out of his hold and pointed frantically back the way she had come. "It is George. I found him on the path. He has been wounded."

Already several of the men had started out in the direction she indicated. Garek shoved her gently toward the keep steps.

"Stay here."

Turning, he ran after his men, his long legs closing the distance between them. Before long he returned, the young lad in his arms and Loup running beside him.

Brianna hadn't moved. Now she flew to Garek's side.

"Get Alfred," Garek commanded.

Brianna hastened to obey. When she returned, she found Garek and his men, in full battle gear, mounting their horses. Brianna's questioning eyes sought an answer from Garek's grim visage.

"Sir Hormis and Earl Waverly have been attacked. The boy managed to make it back here, but we know not if he will survive the day. As for the earl and Sir Hormis. . ."

The gleam in his eyes told Brianna that Garek's revenge would be swift and final, should he find the perpetrators of this deed.

Brianna went back inside where she found a distraught Marie crying faintly by the fire. Brianna went to her, pulling a stool to her side.

"What will I do?" she questioned Brianna, who wasn't sure how to answer her.

"Shall we pray, my lady?"

Marie sniffed into her handkerchief, which she clutched as though it were a lifeline. She turned wet green eyes on Brianna. Slowly she nodded her head.

Softly, Brianna began to talk with the Lord. She prayed for the lives of those involved, and she asked for courage, should there be unfortunate news. Brianna could feel Marie start to relax. As she finished her petition, she rose to her feet, smiling down at the younger girl.

"It is in God's hands now," she told her.

The waiting seemed an eternity, but finally they heard the watchman cry from the tower. Moments later, Garek and his men rode into the courtyard.

One knight trailed another horse behind his, on which was tied a bundled form that Brianna could see was a man. Her heart dropped, for the figure was swathed from head to foot and draped across the saddle.

Another horse being led held its rider upright, though just barely. As they drew closer, Brianna could see that it was Sir Hormis, blood flowing from a gash in his side.

The men lifted him gently from his saddle, carrying him into the keep. As they passed Marie, who stood at the threshold, they averted their eyes.

Brianna turned to Marie, her compassion reaching out to the other. As the truth dawned, the girl crumpled slowly to the ground.

Garek caught her before she hit the stone steps, lifting her gently in his arms. Brianna followed as he carried her up the stairs to her room. He lay her on the bed, his sympathetic look passing over the girl before he turned to Brianna.

"Tell me when she awakens."

Nodding, Brianna passed him to sit on the edge of the bed.

As Garek left the room he could hear Brianna's soft voice gently coaxing the girl to awaken. Lips pressed tightly together, he went to deal with things below.

When Marie came down the stairs later, helped by Brianna's supporting arm, her beautiful green eyes were rimmed in red. Though her face was slightly puffy from crying, that did not detract from her appearance. Her hair, freed from its normal confinement, flowed in bright disarray about her shoulders and down her back, its dark auburn color giving color to her otherwise pale face.

Brianna had wanted her to remain in her room, but the girl was anxious to find out what had happened to her father.

Garek's eyes flicked from one to the other before he went and helped Marie into a chair by the fire. She smiled her appreciation, and Brianna dropped her eyes as a jealous pain pierced her own heart.

Telling Marie the story as gently as possible, Garek watched the girl for some sign of returning hysteria. Instead, her large green eyes regarded him with a wisdom he hadn't known she possessed.

"What will happen now?" she asked.

"If it is to your agreement, I will bury your father on the hill alongside others from this manor who have been laid to rest there."

She nodded her head in agreement.

"The priest will come in the morning to bless the grave," he told her.

"Many thanks, milord," she answered softly.

Garek cleared his throat. "It is understood that you must be allowed your period of mourning. After that. . .after that we shall wed."

Knowing that it was coming did nothing to stop the pain Brianna felt. She longed to go somewhere alone and cry her heart out, but that would accomplish nothing. Marie needed her, and for that matter, so did Garek, for in serving Marie, she was serving him.

The blank look had returned to Marie's face. She lowered her eyes to the floor, but said nothing.

"On the morrow," Garek told her, "we will seek out those who are responsible for this and they will be punished. I have sent word to King William."

Garek's eyes met Brianna's briefly before he left the room.

As darkness descended, Mary began to lay the evening meal. Although she had considered the earl a traitor, her sympathetic look strayed from time to time to his daughter.

Marie sat staring into the fire with trancelike fascination. Periodically, a long sigh would reach across to Brianna, where she knelt to stir the flames.

"Brianna?"

Brianna smiled up at the young serving girl. "What is it, Anne?"

"Alfred has asked that you come. The knight is not doing well, and he has need of your help."

Rising swiftly to her feet, Brianna followed the girl from the room. Alfred often asked her help with his patients, for he well knew that Brianna had skill that he did not. The last words heard by the dying were about the love of Jesus.

When she entered the chamber, she found Alfred bent over his patient, a worried expression on his face.

"He has lost much blood. I am afraid he may not survive."

Brianna went to his side. As she looked down on the young knight, he briefly opened his eyes and stared into hers. His pleading look touched Brianna's heart.

"Sir Hormis," she greeted him. "Pray, how do you feel?"

He smiled weakly. "I have felt better," he muttered hoarsely before closing his eyes again.

Alfred rose to his feet. "There is nothing more I can do for him. I will return on the morrow to see how he fared the night, unless you send me word otherwise."

When he had closed the door behind him, Brianna sat on

the bed next to the young knight. Taking his hand into hers, she closed her eyes and began to pray.

❧

Garek returned to the castle after seeing to Earl Waverly's burial. The priest had been summoned and the grave blessed. Now he had only to consider the rest of his duty.

He mounted the stairs to his bed chamber, for some reason reluctant to enter. Aggravated with himself, he pushed open the door and made his way slowly across the room. He dropped into a chair, exhausted, and began to rub his face with his hands. He leaned back, closing his eyes.

*Deuce, but I am tired.* Since some time before he had returned from London, he had not had a single night's uninterrupted sleep. Each night the dream returned, leaving him in total darkness. There was no longer any source of light. Had he shut himself off from it by his commitment to this marriage?

His honor would not allow him to think of one woman when he was committed to another. He pounded his fist against the arm of the chair. How could he not think of her when she was in the same abode as he, her very presence the first thing he searched for each morning?

He pondered his dilemma.

William would insist on this marriage, he was sure, for he and the earl had been old and dear friends. And in truth, Garek felt honor bound to offer the damsel his protection since he had failed her father.

But what of Brianna? Garek ground his teeth. How had the wench so wrapped herself into his thoughts, his life, and yes, even his heart? Never had he known a woman like her. At first he had thought her a weak, pitiable creature afraid of her own shadow. But then she had saved his life, suffered abuse, interceded for the people of this shire, and even tried to befriend his future wife.

A stronger woman he had yet to meet, and he knew strength came to her from above. He longed to possess such strength, for in comparison, he was the weakling.

He had thought she had feelings for him but now he wasn't so sure. Could a woman who loved a man just hand him over to another woman? He thought not, for he knew such generosity would be beyond him.

Did she care? If not, perhaps he could more easily free his mind of her. Getting to his feet, he pressed his lips tightly together. He would find out. Now.

When he went to Brianna's room, he found it empty. Even the pup was missing. Heart skipping a beat, he searched until he found her in Sir Hormis's room. She was gently stroking the hair from his forehead and talking to him as though he were awake.

"How fares he?"

Brianna jumped at his voice. Her eyelashes flew downward, but not before Garek had a chance to read what was in her eyes.

"He is as well as can be expected," she told him.

Garek realized that now was not the time to press his question. He studied the young knight's face a moment before fastening his gaze once again upon Brianna.

"Tell me if there is any change."

"Yea, milord."

He continued to watch her, but she refused to lift her eyes to his face. Finally, he left.

Brianna breathed a sigh of relief. The look in Garek's eyes had bothered her, for it caused her to hope for things she knew could not be. Was it possible that he really cared for her?

The door creaked open slowly and Brianna felt her heart give a lurch, but it was only Marie.

"I thought perhaps you might permit me to sit with Sir Hormis," she suggested. "Mary seems beside herself, and I am afraid I am not much good in the kitchen. I thought perhaps I would relieve you here, and you could return to your other duties."

Smiling warmly, Brianna motioned her into the room.

"It would please me much," she told the girl. "There is naught to be done save watch for a change."

Marie's scrutiny took in the color of Hormis's face and his still figure. "Will he live?"

"It is in God's hands," Brianna told her.

Something flickered in the girl's eyes before she seated herself beside the bed. "Yea," she said tonelessly.

For a moment Brianna was tempted to challenge the girl, but then she remembered that those had been the precise words she had used regarding the girl's father. Reasoning with her now would not be advisable, because she needed time to overcome her own pain.

Brianna returned to the kitchen and began to help Mary prepare the evening meal. Although Mary looked harassed, Brianna realized that she didn't seem brokenhearted. What then were her feelings for Sir Hormis?

"How fares the knight?" she asked, and Brianna searched her face for signs of distress. She returned Brianna's look, her eyes full of compassion, but nothing more.

"Only time will tell."

Though she was concerned, Brianna could see that Mary was not unduly distressed by Sir Hormis's condition.

After the evening meal, Brianna went to her favorite place in the garden to think. She pulled her shawl close against the cool night air, studying the stars above her.

It was said by some that the stars guided one's destiny. The brilliant glowing lights in the sky twinkled reassuringly back at her. *Nay,* she thought, *I know who guides my fate, I just don't know His plans concerning me.*

Garek found her seated on a wooden bench, her head thrown back, eyes closed. He hesitated to make his presence known, for there was such a look of peace on her face. It was clear to him that Brianna had been speaking again with the Lord. Garek was awed by her ability to do so.

For as long as he could remember, only the priests and nuns had dared to speak so familiarly about God, or to Him. It was considered blasphemous to do so. He was a little afraid of Brianna at such times, for it was obvious from the light in her eyes that she did indeed commune with the Lord.

Sensing a presence, she turned his way, rising swiftly to her feet when she realized who it was.

"Milord? Am I needed?"

Waving his hand, he motioned her to return to her seat. "Nay, I wanted only to speak with you."

He crossed to her side, staring intently down at her. "You were speaking with God?"

Alerted by something in his manner, she watched him as she answered him carefully.

"Yea."

Various thoughts chased across his features, though Brianna could not seize any of them in the dim light.

He sat down next to her on the bench, turning his face upward. "Would that I could do the same."

"But Garek, you may. God wants all to call on Him. He wants to be your Father as well as your God."

His look searched her face. "It is not proper for someone like me to do so."

"Someone like you? You are as much a child of God as anyone. He loves you. He wants to forgive you and be your Father, but He cannot do that unless you first realize your own sins and confess them to Him."

Garek snorted. "My sins are too many to confess. It would take all night, and then some."

"Then so be it," she told him softly.

He shook his head, frowning. "Nay. It cannot be that simple."

"But it is. Your sins are no greater than others'."

He took her hand and she felt her pulse leap in response. He must have noticed, for his eyes went swiftly to her face.

"What great sins could you possibly have committed?" he

asked, his voice low and husky.

"We have all sinned, Garek. I am no saint, so do not mistake me for one. Even men chosen by the Lord Himself were not without guilt."

She tried to pull her hand away, but he would not release it.

"I did not realize what I was missing in life until I met you," he told her, pulling her hand to his lips. The warm pressure against her skin sent the blood rushing through her body.

This time she jerked her hand away and rose to her feet.

"I must go in now," she told him in a quavery voice.

He took her wrist, keeping her in place. Standing, he bent forward until his face was close to hers.

One large hand wrapped gently around the back of her neck. "Nay, Brianna. The time for fleeing is past."

He pulled her into his strong arms, his lips pressed hungrily against hers. For a moment she remained motionless in his arms, returning his kiss, for this was where she yearned to be.

But then reality returned, and with it, thoughts of the beautiful young woman waiting inside who would one day be this man's bride. She began to struggle, pulling her lips away.

"Nay, Garek! Unhand me!"

Garek loosened his hold, but refused to relinquish his possession.

"Do you deny that you love me?" He shook her slightly. "Do you?"

She shook her head from side to side. "Nay, but you are betrothed. Have you forgotten?"

Finally he released her and they stood face to face, both breathing raggedly.

Garek's eyes glittered with some inner fire. "Yea, I had forgotten."

Brianna could see his struggle as he tried to regain control of himself. Pushing past him, she fled to the safety of the keep, and this time, he let her go.

## nine

Brianna paced up and down in her bed chamber, her agitation evident as she chewed nervously on her bottom lip. She had to leave. She couldn't possibly stay, for if Garek ever decided to push his suit, she was not sure how long she could hold him off; and it was possible that Garek, and yes, even she herself, would betray all that they both believed in.

Laughing without mirth, Brianna felt her own shame. Often she had chided the women in this shire for their fleshly desires, warning them of possible consequences, and yet here she was for the first time in her life experiencing the same thing.

Where Garek was concerned, she had little willpower with which to resist. She had not believed Mary when Mary had told her that when a woman loves a man, she becomes his pawn. Her own love would make her a slave if she were not careful. She would not, could not, betray her Lord.

Throwing herself to the floor beside Loup, Brianna absently stroked the dog's fur.

"What can I do, Loup? I cannot stay here, but I am forbidden to leave the manor."

Loup whined softly, nuzzling her hand with his muzzle. Brianna smiled down at him.

"And what of you? Who would take care of you? Mary, perhaps, but I do not think you would stay, would you, my friend?"

Brianna decided that her only course of action for the moment was to stay as far from Garek as possible.

◆

Brianna studied the young knight lying motionless in the bed. She wished there was more she could do for him besides pray, but there was not.

Leaning forward, she removed the cloth from Hormis's fevered brow and replaced it with a fresh, cooler one. She shifted her weight in the chair, her tired muscles rebelling at this inactivity.

How long had she been sitting here? Her rumbling stomach told her it was long past time for the noon meal. Had Mary forgotten to bring her a tray, or was she too busy?

The door creaked open and Marie Waverly entered, balancing a tray across her arm. Brianna rose and took the food from her, allowing Marie to close the door behind her.

"How is he today?" she asked, nodding her head toward Hormis.

"There has been no change," Brianna told her. "But he is no worse, either."

"I will sit with him later, if you wish."

Brianna smiled at the girl. Although Brianna was only a few years older than Marie, she felt immeasurably older. Brianna welcomed the fact that the two had become friends when so much was against them. It was hard not to like Marie.

"I would very much appreciate that, Marie. Mary has too much to attend to as it is."

Smiling slightly, Marie left Brianna to her meal. As she ate, Brianna let her mind wander. She hadn't encountered Garek yet this day and her mind balked at the idea of approaching him about leaving the manor. His temper was unpredictable at the best of times; what would he be like if she dared suggest she must leave?

Garek seemed to have developed a fixation upon her as his only means of salvation. She had tried repeatedly to tell him of the Lord's love for him and that he need only accept the Lord's offer to be his Father.

Garek just could not understand this, believing himself unforgivable. What pain that must cause a man who wanted peace so badly.

When Marie returned later, Brianna took her tray and went to the kitchen. Mary was nowhere to be found, so Brianna set about preparing the evening meal. With so many men to feed, it seemed she and Mary were constantly providing food.

She prepared a special broth that she hoped she could feed to Sir Hormis, setting it aside to cool. The young knight was fighting for his life and Brianna was determined to help him as much as possible.

Brianna climbed the stairs, carefully holding the bowl of broth. She was not aware of Garek's presence until he was standing before her on the steps.

They looked at each other a long moment before Garek indicated the bowl. "For Hormis?"

"Yea," she answered, unable to form a coherent sentence. Last night's scene still played over and over in her mind, bringing a blush to her cheeks.

Garek smiled slightly at the telltale color. Moving aside, he allowed her to continue her ascent. Brianna could feel his eyes watching her, but she refused to look around.

Brianna found Marie sitting quietly, busily employed with her needlework. She smiled at Brianna.

"Would you like me to try to feed him some broth when he wakes?"

Surprised, Brianna looked from one to the other. "Has he awakened?"

Marie nodded. "A few times, but he does not stay awake long."

Brianna smiled widely. "It is a good sign. I will stay and watch now, if you have other things to attend to."

"Nay," Marie told her. "I have nothing else to keep me occupied."

Watching the girl, Brianna couldn't help but feel for her. What must it be like to have no duties to perform, no tasks to make life worthwhile? Marie was not yet lady of this manor, nor could she call any other place home. Brianna realized

Marie must feel as though she had nowhere to belong and no one to turn to. Perhaps that was why Brianna felt herself so drawn to the girl.

"Let me know as soon as Sir Hormis awakens, will you?" Brianna asked.

Garek was waiting for her outside the door.

"I wish to speak with you."

Brianna studied his face, but it gave away nothing of his thoughts or feelings. She followed him into his bed chamber, very aware of the precariousness of the situation. Still, Garek was lord of this manor, and as such, his word was law.

Garek closed the door behind them and Brianna felt her stomach give a lurch. Trying to curb her feelings, she turned a blank stare toward Garek.

"Yea, milord?"

He leaned his back against the door, his hands behind him. He stayed that way so long, Brianna felt her own resolve to control her feelings give way. She was more nervous than she could ever remember being in his presence.

When he moved away from the door, Brianna hurried to put between them the huge hand-carved table that Garek had added to the rather spartan chamber. Even it seemed a rather flimsy barrier, but she felt the need for something.

Garek placed his palms on the table, leaning forward and impaling her with his glance.

"We must needs get this settled between us," he told her, his voice raspy.

"There is nothing to settle, milord. There is nothing between us."

Garek looked down at the table separating them, one eyebrow winging upward as his look returned to her face. "What is between us is more than this flimsy table. We must settle this, Brianna, or I will go mad."

Brianna shrugged her shoulders helplessly. "Garek, you are betrothed. Yea, I have feelings for you, but they can come to naught." Leaning forward, she beseeched him with her eyes. "Let me leave this manor."

Garek reared back as though he had been struck. His gray eyes grew icy with suppressed anger. "Never."

"Then what would you suggest, milord?"

His voice came back soft, evocative. "I would suggest that you come out from behind that table and let us discuss this more thoroughly."

Brianna took a step backward, vehemently shaking her head.

A grin tugged at Garek's mouth. "You do not trust me?"

Again that shake of the head. "Nay, nor do I trust myself."

Growing weary of the game, Garek moved around the table, but Brianna moved as quickly in the opposite direction.

"Brianna!"

The message in Garek's eyes sent a fire tingling all the way to her toes.

"Garek, this is no game we are playing at!"

"Yea, you think I know it not?"

Reaching out a hand, Brianna unconsciously pleaded with him. "Think of Marie."

Before answering, Garek's hand snatched and took Brianna's wrist. Gently he began tugging her toward him. He could see the fear leap into her eyes, and it gave him pause. Was she really afraid of him?

When she was finally standing before him, Garek could see that she was trembling. Lifting a hand, he stroked the back of it along her cheek.

"I do not wish to harm you, Brianna. I only want to hold you."

"Nay, Garek," she whispered. "It is not right. You belong to another."

"Nay, ma cherie," he told her. "I belong only to you."

Jerking her head up, she stared at him in surprise. What was he saying? What about his betrothal? Marie had no one and could not just be set aside.

"What of Marie?"

Garek shook his head, closing his palms around her face. "I will think of something. I will not give you up."

When his lips came down on hers, Brianna allowed him his moment. Already her mind was forming a plan, and she knew this could be the last kiss she ever received from Garek. She gave him kiss for kiss, then pulled herself free of his arms.

"I must go and see to Sir Hormis," she told him breathlessly, keeping her eyes on the plank floor.

"Yea," he answered softly. "Perhaps that would be best." He watched her cross the room and open the door.

Before she could leave, he told her, "I am taking some men and I will try to find those who have murdered Earl Waverly. When I return, we will discuss this further."

"Yea, milord."

Some time later, Brianna watched from Hormis's window as the men rode away, her heart aching with longing. She had thought she was destined to never know a woman's love for a man, and now that she had, it brought nothing but pain.

Garek had given his oath to William, and again to Marie Waverly. The Scriptures taught that an oath should never be entered into unless you were willing to fulfill it. To break an oath was a sin, and Brianna could not bear to bring that disgrace upon Garek.

Climbing the stairs to her room, Brianna sat on her bed. When Loup climbed up beside her, she wrapped her arms around his neck.

Her heart was heavy, but it had to be done. She had to leave this place, and she now knew where she could flee. Picking up her cloak, she tied a rope to Loup's neck and left.

❧

"What say you?"

Garek tried to control his rage as Mary trembled on her knees before him. It was not the girl's fault, but he needed to vent his fury.

"I tell you she is gone. No one has seen her for two days." Fear twisted Garek's insides as he thought of the possible consequences of Brianna's action. Wolves ranged the countryside, and not all of them were of the four-legged variety.

Calming himself, Garek reached down and gently pulled the quaking girl to her feet. Two days! Garek regretted now that he had decided to follow his quarry until he found them. Yes, he did find them, and thankfully they had chosen to fight, because Garek had no idea what form his punishment would have taken otherwise. But due to his tarrying, Brianna had two days head start on him, and he had no idea in which direction she'd fled.

His anger flared anew. When he got his hands on the girl, she would pay dearly for causing him such anguish. Turning, Garek strode to the door leading to the courtyard. Bellowing for his knights, he awaited their answer to his summons.

Barough was the first to reach Garek's side.

"Gather some of the men. Brianna is lost."

Eyes wide, Barough hastened to obey. The men gathered in the courtyard, awaiting Garek's instructions.

Triden handed Garek the reins to his horse and together they mounted. With a clatter of hooves they exited the castle courtyard.

Garek sent his men in all directions, knowing they would do their best to find the maid, for each loved her in his own way. Faces intent, they scoured the ground for clues.

Darkness was descending when the men returned to the castle, their faces pinched with their failure. Garek alone remained mounted as his men dismounted and made their way into the great hall.

Marie Waverly stood in the open doorway, her concerned face lifted to his in question.

"We have not found her," he told her, his voice devoid of emotion. "I will continue the search as soon as Sir Barough brings me some provisions."

Barough returned to his side, handing Garek the provender he had requested. His worried eyes searched Garek's face.

"It is not good to be out after dark, my liege. It is not safe, even for a knight such as you. Bands of brigands still tread our shire."

One look into Garek's eyes convinced Barough that any man who crossed Garek's path with less than honorable intentions was a fool.

Reining his steed about, Garek was quickly out of sight.

❧

Each day, Garek sent his men out riding in an ever widening circle to cover the land about him. Querying the villeins in the vicinity brought no information. Brianna seemed to have disappeared without a trace.

At night, Garek slumped into his chair nursing a mug of ale. His demeanor kept even the bravest of souls away from him.

If Marie were afraid of him before, she was terrified of him now. There was no doubt in her mind that Garek loved Brianna. It was all too apparent. It was also apparent that Brianna had fled for that very reason. Did she fear the lord of the manor? Had his attentions become less than honorable? Or did she flee for another reason?

It had been almost a fortnight since Brianna's disappearance and still there had been no word. Garek fought the deep depression he found himself sinking into. It was becoming more and more reasonable to assume that something terrible had happened to Brianna. Garek's only reassurance was that she had taken her dog with her. The beast had grown huge in the half-year duration of his life.

Garek found Brianna's favorite spot in the garden and seated himself on the stone where she normally perched. He lifted his eyes heavenward. Did he dare? What had he to lose? He was half dead anyway.

Clearing his throat, he hesitantly spoke his thoughts aloud.

"Great God of Heaven. . ." He stopped, unable to go on. What did one say to the Creator of the universe? How did Brianna do it?

Finally Garek bowed his head and let his anguish speak for him. In the end, he found he needed no words. The agony of his soul spoke for him. He pleaded for her life, that she would be safe. He promised to treat her more honorably in the future. And he begged for her to be returned to him.

When he opened his eyes again, he was exhausted. Getting slowly to his feet, he sluggishly made his way back to the keep. He knew he had been heard as surely as he knew the stars were twinkling overhead. But, would his prayers be answered?

࡚

The watchman shouted his warning early the next morning. A lone rider approached. The guard opened the gate, giving them an indication that the visitor was known.

Garek regarded Sir Bolson making his way slowly up the hill toward him. There was no smile on either man's face as each remembered their parting.

Bolson stopped in front of Garek, his eyes trying to gauge the older knight's reaction.

"Sir Bolson," Garek acknowledged. "What brings you to our shire?"

Bolson hadn't missed the fact that there had been no welcome in Garek's greeting.

"King William sent me."

Surprised, Garek watched as Bolson dismounted. Handing the reins to a villein standing nearby, Bolson turned back to Garek.

"I have come, also, to apologize."

Garek said nothing, though his face relaxed. Reaching out a hand, Garek waited for Bolson to take his arm. They clasped each other's forearms.

"I have been a fool," Garek told his friend. "And you were the only one who was wise enough to see it."

A grin lifted one corner of Bolson's mouth. "Nay, my liege. Not wise. I was the only one fool enough to question you."

Garek returned his smile with one of his own. "Nay, you were the only one brave enough to tell me the truth, and I turned on you. I fear I had no desire to face the truth."

Bolson followed Garek into the keep, his eyes searching the main hall. His look fastened on Mary, standing demurely by the doorway to the cooking chamber. She dropped her eyes, her face coloring hotly.

Garek turned to his friend. "You have heard about Earl Waverly and Sir Hormis?"

Bolson nodded. "Aye, it is why William has sent me. He wishes me to inform you that he will be here within the month to help preside over your wedding to Marie Waverly."

The look that crossed Garek's face was not lost on his friend. "He said to spare no expense. We are to give the people of England something to celebrate, something to take their minds off of war and destruction."

Bolson glanced quickly around the room. "He also says to tell you to begin work on a new castle—a stone castle, to repel invaders."

Garek snorted. "Had England done so in the beginning, perhaps this land would still belong to them. Yea, it is wise of William to so protect his throne."

Sir Bolson continued to watch the people entering and leaving the chamber. Garek noticed his interest.

"Are you seeking someone in particular, Sir Bolson?"

"Yea. I was wondering where Brianna was."

This was the very thing that had caused the breach in their friendship before. Garek's eyes grew cold. *Has Bolson decided that since William is coming to see I am wed, now is the time to claim Brianna? He can think again!*

He had another thought. *Could Bolson be the answer to my prayer? Has God intended this from the beginning?* Quailing at the thought, Garek turned to anger to ease his pain.

"Brianna is gone."

Swiveling back to face him, Bolson's face registered surprise. "Gone? Where?"

The room grew strangely quiet. Garek shoved one hand back through his blond hair. "No one knows."

Bolson's surprise was followed by dread, and then anger of his own. "What say you, no one knows? How can this be?"

"She left," Garek told him flatly. "Without telling anyone. Not even Mary."

Bolson glared at Garek a long moment before turning and heading for the door.

"Where are you going?" Garek demanded.

"To find her."

"It is what we have tried to do for a fortnight now."

Bolson turned in frustration. "I will not come back until I have found her."

"And what then?"

Bolson glowered back at him, "And then I intend to marry her."

Whirling about, he left the room.

# ten

Brianna knelt on the cold stone floor and stared across the room at the woman seated at the table before her. Brianna had confessed all, and the abbess only smiled gently with no evidence of reproof.

"Perhaps, Brianna, it is God's way of bringing you back to service for Him."

Frowning in confusion, Brianna shook her head slightly. "I fear I do not understand what you are saying."

The abbess leaned back in her chair. "Women who enter the Lord's service give up much to do so. The only love they will ever know is the love of the people they serve. It is not enough for some, and they seek more elsewhere."

Brianna nodded. She understood that well, because no matter how much she had believed a man could never love her, she had hungered for it. Now, having known that feeling and realizing it could never be hers, the thought of giving her whole life to God was not so frightening.

Speaking more to herself than to the other woman, Brianna asked softly, "What is it, Mother, that makes a woman choose one man out of all the men of the world? And the same for a man? What makes people see only each other when there are others more fair, or more handsome?" She was thinking of Edward's wife Ruina, who, although beautiful beyond comparison, had chosen Edward, who could only be described as plain.

They had been so happy together. Ruina had adored her husband, and Edward had been gentle, kind, and loving, both as a husband and a father. Only after the death of wife and child had Edward changed.

And what of Garek? Why did he seek out Brianna when he had the beautiful Marie right at his fingertips? And out of all the available men, why had it been the dark knight who had so touched Brianna's heart?

Smiling with understanding, the nun answered softly, "It is a miracle of God that man cannot explain. Perhaps God Himself finds us our mates if we will only listen when He calls us to them. But one must listen with the heart and not just with the body."

Coming from one who had denounced such worldly things, Brianna was amazed at the woman's understanding.

The nun's look hardened, if that were possible of such a gentle lady. "Brianna, you cannot hide from love. If that is what you seek to do, then you cannot stay here."

Brianna dropped her eyes so that the sister would not see the guilt she felt was surely residing there. "I seek only time to know God's will for my life. I have always wished to do only His will."

Getting up from her chair, the abbess crossed to Brianna and placed a hand lovingly on her lowered head. "I know, child. It has always been your way. Even after so many years away from us, your light still shines as brightly as ever."

In light of the past few months, Brianna questioned the truth of the statement. She felt as though she had let the Lord down terribly. "Then I may stay, Mother?"

The nun hesitated only a moment before removing her hand and returning to her seat behind the table. "Yea, Brianna. You may stay. For a time. But I wish you to listen for God's leading in your life."

Sighing with relief, Brianna rose from her knees. "Thank you, Mother."

Making her way to the garden, Brianna tried to squelch her feelings of unhappiness. The happiest times of her life had been behind these cloistered walls, and she was seeking the peace that seemed to have fled from her.

Loup whined when she entered the small courtyard. Brianna's heart constricted at his downcast expression. He had never been tied before and he didn't understand the restriction now. It was only by the abbess's grace that he had been allowed to stay at all.

She went to him, kneeling beside him and stroking his fur. "What else could I do? I dared not leave you behind, for you would have led them straight to me."

Her thoughts were in turmoil. Would Garek seek her out? Would he even care that she was gone? Part of her hoped that he would, the other part firmly berated her for wishing such a thing.

Would anyone else miss her? Maybe Mary. Brianna felt a twinge of remorse, realizing that she was probably causing her friend anguish. The two of them had been close for many years, ever since Mary's father had been brought to the convent to recover from some strange illness that had made others in the village so afraid, they had wanted to kill him.

The nuns had cared for him, as they did anyone who had need of a place to stay. It was during this time that Brianna and Mary had become fast friends. Mary came to see her father every day, and although she would have cared for him probably as well as the nuns, she realized he was better protected at the convent.

This had been at the time Brianna was going through her period of novitiate—preparation to become a full Benedictine nun. She never finished that training, though, for Edward removed her from the convent, saying he had need of her.

She had felt it her duty to go, especially since Edward's family had been killed in such an appalling way. She had wanted to help Edward by giving him both her help and her love. The one he accepted, the other he fiercely rejected.

Brianna watched him change overnight from a loving, gentle man to a vengeful monster with no care for human life. Often he took his anger out on her, and at times she had fled to Mary for a respite from his anger.

She had considered returning to the convent but she was afraid of what Edward might do, for he had no fear of God or the church and rejected anything they might stand for. Perhaps that was why she angered him so much, because even in the most trying times, she always went to her Lord for help and comfort.

Now she had a chance to finish her novitiate, but she knew it would only happen if she could convince Garek to allow it. The abbess would not allow her to do so unless she received permission from the lord of the manor.

But would he grant her that permission? Certainly not at this moment. Perhaps in time, if the abbess first talked with him as she had suggested.

Getting to her feet, she took Loup's lead and led him to the outer courtyard for some exercise. How would she convince the good sisters to allow Loup to sleep in her cell with her? She needed him, more than ever now.

&

The ominous sheen of Garek's eyes gave Bolson pause, but Bolson's own anger was past endurance. His frustration at having been unable to locate Brianna added to his already frayed temper.

"As part of this manor, Brianna belongs to me. What makes you think I will give her over to you?"

Bolson held his ground. "This manor is yours by King William's leave. It actually belongs to him."

"It is the same thing."

Bolson shook his head. "Nay, Garek. Not so. I have spoken with William about Brianna, and he has decided to give her to me."

Before he was aware of what was happening, Bolson was lifted from the floor by Garek's mighty hands, his toes scraping the planks beneath him. Garek had raised a huge fist in readiness to strike when Marie entered the room.

Her eyes popped open wide, her face drained of color. Giving a frightened shriek, she fled from the room.

Bolson's hands hung limply at his sides, for he refused to fight his liege and friend. He well understood Garek's anger, but Garek needed to be made to understand a few things as well.

Garek blinked his eyes at the now empty doorway, the killing fire of his anger cooling somewhat. Slowly he released Bolson from his grasp.

The younger knight straightened his clothes, his gaze never leaving Garek's face.

"Be gone before I kill you." Garek's voice was softly menacing.

"Garek, listen to me. You are my friend."

Murderous gray eyes turned his way. "Pull your sword now and I will give lie to your words."

Bolson sighed. Perhaps now was not the time to speak, but if not now, he might never be able to have his say. Even in such a rage, surely Garek could be made to see reason.

"Will you marry Brianna yourself?" he asked.

A low growl came from the huge knight. "It is none of your affair."

"I disagree," Bolson continued, undaunted by the obvious threat to his own life. "Cannot you see how many lives will be affected by this. . .this whole affair? Will you break your vow to William? To Marie Waverly?" Helplessly, he held out his arms at his sides. "Think, Garek. Will you marry Marie and keep Brianna as your mistress?"

Garek took a step toward Bolson, his hands clenching at his sides, but Bolson continued.

"Would you do that to Brianna? Would you? I have seen the love she has for you. Will she give herself willingly to you when you are married to another?"

Garek restrained his fury with difficulty. Slowly, Bolson's words penetrated the red hot haze of his anger. Could he break his vow to William? To Marie? Could he make Brianna so forget herself and her honor that she would come to him anyway, whether he was married or not? The thought made his blood run hot, then swiftly turn to ice.

He looked Bolson in the eye, both men sending and receiving messages.

"Why do you want her?" Garek asked softly.

Bolson dropped his eyes. How could he make Garek see? Brianna was everything a man could truly desire in a woman. Kind, gentle, honest, giving. A man could rule the world with such a woman by his side, not that he had such aspirations himself.

"I do not wish to see her hurt."

"You do not love her."

Bolson sighed. "In my own way I do."

Mary entered the room, laying a trencher of meat on the trellis table. Her eyes were rimmed in red, evidence of a recent weep.

Both men watched her silently until she retreated from the room. Garek turned to his friend.

"I thought your desires ran elsewhere."

"I told you once before: I am a man, not some boy to play games with."

The silence grew uncomfortably long between them. Finally Garek spoke, and his words had the ring of steel.

"Regardless of what William has promised you, you will not have her."

Bolson lifted his mantle from the stool before the fire. He gave back glare for glare. "Tell it to William when he arrives in a fortnight. Yea, Garek. Tell it to him."

Garek watched Bolson leave, his own emotions in a tangle. He had loved the younger knight as one would a younger brother. But now he felt like slaying him with his own hands. What was this curious mixture of pride in the lad, and murderous intent toward him? Bolson had grown strong and proud.

Now that he had dared to challenge Garek, what would be next?

&

Brianna smiled at the young lad standing before her, twisting his cap nervously in his hands. His head was bowed in shame.

"It is no shame to need help, Andrew," she told him quietly. "Everyone needs help at one time or another."

He glanced at her. "Yea, Brianna, but it is hard to do so when you are strong and can easily work."

"Have you talked to the lord of the manor?"

The lad's face twisted in anger. "Bah! I would rather be like Beowulf and slay him in his castle." Seeing the look on her face, he relented. "I am sorry, Brianna."

Trying to keep her feelings to herself, Brianna asked him, "You see Lord Garek as Grendel, then?"

"Aye. All Normans."

Brianna sighed. "Lord Garek is no monster, Andrew. He is a good man, and generous. You would do well to seek him out and tell him of your needs."

The lad's lips set mutinously. "I would rather die!"

"And Jenna with you?"

Andrew's shoulders sagged, and Brianna knew she had scored a point. "She is with child now, is she not?"

"Aye."

"And you would wish your own son dead as well?"

He glared back at her in impotent rage. Brianna shook her head gently. "It is time for us to put aside our differences and turn to the work of living instead of dying. Remember, Andrew, that King William has the blessing of the church."

Andrew's face paled as the truth of what she said set in. To fight against William was to fight against the church itself.

Brianna handed the lad the sack she had prepared for him. He took it reluctantly.

"There are enough vegetables and bread to last you several days." She took the lad's hand gently into her own. "Go to Lord Garek, Andrew. Tell him what a strong worker you are.

Give him a chance. Give King William a chance."

Nodding his bowed head, he left.

Brianna returned to the garden where she had been working. Many of the nuns were already hard at work weeding and picking. The convent grew enough vegetables to feed themselves and still help others.

Only those who took the simple perpetual vows worked the gardens and helped in the hospital. Those who took solemn vows spent their time only in prayer and meditation.

Brianna knew that, for her, joy came from helping others, and that if she took her vows, they would be simple ones. She was reluctant to think on the matter much now, because she knew that once she made the commitment, there would be no turning back.

Brianna spent most of her time in quiet meditation, reflecting on God's love for her—but more often on her own love for Garek. Try as she might, she could not shake his image from her mind. Already three weeks had passed since she had fled the castle, but her memories would not dim. Even now her lips tingled when she thought of Garek's kisses.

She helped the nuns around the convent but many of them had very little to say to her. Some were truly pious, others were biding their time until their wealthy families would free them from monastic life to be joined in marriage to some landed gentleman.

Brianna's one solace was her dog, Loup. She showered on him all the love she had stored inside her, and the beast grew under her care.

Thinking herself safe from Garek's searching, Brianna had taken to going for walks along the bank of the river that flowed through the village and past the manor. Although the convent was close to the manor, it was secluded and rarely visited.

Brianna needed the exercise as well, but she took the walks mainly for Loup's benefit. She watched the dog with loving eyes, his huge form well rounded from good food and exercise. She wondered briefly about his breeding, realizing by his size and stature that he must have some wolf in his blood-line. It was hard to remember him as that scrawny little pup she had spent hours coaxing to drink from the glove finger.

Entering the woods that ran parallel to the river, Brianna sighed as she took a deep breath of the rich loam of the forest floor. The musky scent filled her with satisfaction. She had always loved the forest and had never been afraid to venture there.

The sun shone brightly, sending its warming rays peeking through the limbs of the forest trees. The warmth of the sun enhanced the loamy scent pervading the air around her.

The foreboding silence finally penetrated her musings and she felt the hair tingle along the back of her neck. Something was not right. All sounds within the forest seemed to have ceased.

Loup had stopped his own gamboling and now stood alert, ears forward, his nose testing the scents on the faint breeze that so gently stirred the leaves on the trees. Rustlings in the underbrush warned them of something moving their way.

Brianna felt herself frozen to the spot, fear worming its way through her body. Shaking her head, she scolded herself. *What have I to fear in these woods so close to the convent? Surely nothing could harm me here. It was probably some small animal that was as frightened of me as I was of it.*

The hair rose on the back of Loup's neck and a slow rumble began to come from deep within his chest. When a huge animal lunged from the cover of the forest, Brianna was unprepared. Jerking herself back, she twisted her ankle and fell to the ground.

A massive black wolf glared menacingly at her, white froth foaming from its mouth. Snarling and growling, it began to stagger toward her, its tongue swollen and hanging from gaping jaws.

Brianna's eyes widened in real fear, for unless she was very mistaken, this beast had the foaming sickness that made animals and men alike run mad.

Loup's low growls turned to snarls of warning that the animal was too mindless to heed. Loup could not possibly win such a conflict, for although he was a large dog, he was nothing compared to the beast creeping toward Brianna.

Fearing for his safety she commanded him to stay, but for the first time she could remember, the dog paid her no heed. He was intent on protecting his mistress.

Loup launched himself at the wolf, careful to stay a short distance away. He was a smart dog, but he was also committed to defending her. Hearing Loup's growls so close by, the wolf hesitated, his great head swinging toward the dog.

"Nay, Loup. Stay!" Brianna commanded, her voice shrill with fear. She had managed to raise herself to her feet, but she knew she could not outrun the animal. Her ankle had twisted when she fell and now throbbed painfully.

Remembering that those with the madness feared water, Brianna began to inch her way toward the river. At her movement, the wolf's head swung back to her, his vacuous eyes gleaming. He slowly began lumbering toward her again, and without warning Loup catapulted himself at the black beast, his fangs sinking into the wolf's neck.

Squealing in fury, the wolf turned his attack on his assailant. Brianna watched in horror as both animals reared back on their hind legs, their fangs snapping and ripping at each other.

The wolf's sickness had weakened him enough that Loup could hold his own, but the crazy animal fought mindlessly, finally pinning Loup to the ground.

"Nay!" Brianna screamed, trying to move closer to the animals. Her ankle twisted beneath her and she again fell to the ground. Frustrated, she lifted her head in time to see Loup make it to his feet.

Loup, using all the skill his instincts had instilled in him, fought bravely until finally the wolf, weak and tired, fell to the ground.

The dog stood staring at his fallen foe, a slow whine escaping him. Ears twitching, he turned his head to Brianna.

Calling him to her side, Brianna began to cry. "You foolish dog! He could have killed you! You brave, brave dog."

Tears continued flowing down her cheeks as she checked the dogs injuries. Although bloody and torn, he seemed in high spirits.

A low snarl brought Brianna to her feet, and Loup whirling to face his enemy. The bloody wolf staggered toward them again, his now bloody tongue hanging to one side.

Unsure of what to do, Brianna hung onto the leather thong around Loup's neck. Again she tried to back them toward the water, but Loup was reluctant to go. His eyes remained fastened on his opponent.

The wolf tensed his body in preparation for a lunge. Even in his weakened state, the animal's strength was incredible, and he propelled himself unerringly toward them.

Letting out a scream, Brianna instinctively covered her face with her arms, thereby missing the sight of the huge beast impaled in midair by the arrow from a long bow. The sudden sound of horses hooves brought Brianna's head snapping around. She stared wordlessly into Garek's angry gray eyes.

Dismounting, he quickly made his way to the wolf, his lips turning down when he noticed the white foam. Anxious eyes turned Brianna's way.

"You are well?"

Nodding, Brianna let loose her hold on Loup's thong. Deep impressions cut grooves along her palm.

"Loup saved my life," she told him huskily, her knees beginning to quiver like the rustling leaves.

Garek crossed rapidly to her side. "Did the beast bite you?"

Brianna shook her head. "Nay, only Loup."

The look that passed through his eyes as he glanced down at the dog was quickly hidden. "You are certain the animal did not touch you? Not even to scratch you?"

Frowning, Brianna again shook her head. "Nay, I tell you. Only Loup." She reached for the dog's lead. "I must take him and see about his wounds."

Garek took the lead from her nerveless fingers. He motioned to Sir Barough, who was sitting quietly watching the whole scene.

The knight walked his horse over to stand beside them. Garek placed his hands around Brianna's waist and lifted her to the pommel in front of Barough. The two knights exchanged knowing glances.

Turning his horse, Barough headed back to the manor at a swift trot. Confused, Brianna turned her head, trying to see over his shoulder.

"Wait! What are you going to do?"

Neither man answered her. Garek looked down at the dog that was trying to go after Brianna. He held the lead tightly, waiting until the two were nearly out of sight.

Before they rounded the bend, Brianna caught Garek's look, and in that instant, she knew.

"Nay! Garek, nay!"

They were halfway to the castle when Brianna saw the smoke climbing from the woods. Burying her face in her hands, she began to sob uncontrollably. Barough glanced at her bent head and felt her grief. Swallowing hard, he hurried his steed forward. Better to give her over to someone who could deal with her tears; as for him, he could not.

They reached the castle courtyard amid cries from the guardhouse, and Sir Bolson was the first to reach their side. His eyes went wide at the sight of Brianna on the horse, weeping as though her very heart were breaking.

Sir Barough handed Brianna into Sir Bolson's waiting arms, their eyes meeting over her head. "Her dog was bitten by a wolf with the foaming sickness."

When Brianna looked into Bolson's eyes, his were filled with sympathy and gentle understanding. Her own filled with more tears, and laying her head against his shoulder, she allowed him to carry her inside.

## eleven

Garek strode across the courtyard and climbed the stairs to the great hall above. Without hesitation he made his way to the kitchen. Trying to control his temper, he opened the door more quietly than he normally would.

Brianna stood looking out the window and Garek knew she couldn't help but see the billows of black smoke rising from the woods. Mary was at her side, one arm lovingly about Brianna's waist. Both women turned at his entrance.

"Leave us," Garek commanded Mary without taking his eyes from Brianna.

Reluctantly Mary made her way across the room, glancing once at the lord of the manor. His features seemed cast in stone, and Mary hastily retreated from the room.

Closing the door behind her, Garek leaned back against it. "You have been at the convent all of this time?" he asked quietly.

Brianna nodded, turning back to the window.

Garek crossed to her side. His fingers itched to touch her, to make sure she was real. Night after night he had pictured her in his mind until, after nearly a month, he had almost begun to believe she had been a figment of his imagination.

He didn't know what to say. Clearing his throat, he thought to comfort her and assuage his own guilt feelings at the same time.

"I had to kill him. You know that, do you not?"

Tears sprang again to her eyes and she stared at him blankly. He went to take her into his arms, but she pulled away from him.

"Could you not have let me try to save him? He saved my life."

"I am most grateful for that, Brianna. More than you can possibly know. But I could not take the chance. Think of all the children in this shire."

Brianna knew he was right but still felt that the Lord would have spared Loup. "I could have caged him. I could have cleaned and treated his wounds. Maybe he would not have developed the sickness."

This time Garek did take her in his arms, and she buried her face against his chest. They both knew her tears were for more than just the dog, loved though he had been.

Garek nuzzled the top of her head with his chin. "Would you be able to cage him? Could you tolerate seeing him every day pleading for release? And when the sickness came, could you kill him then? Is he not better off this way?"

"Oh, Garek," she cried. It was all she could say. Her heart was sore, her mind numb. Nothing had changed. Everything had changed.

"Macherie," Garek whispered, "lean on my strength."

And for a moment, she did just that. She sniffled into his chest, feeling secure for the first time in a long while. "How did you know where to find me?"

She could feel the chuckle vibrate from his chest. "A certain young villein by the name of Andrew."

She leaned back in surprise, her eyes searching his face. "Andrew came to see you?"

"Aye. He made it quite clear to me his own feelings on the matter, but he said he was not one to go against the church. Was this your doing, m'amoure?"

Brianna shook her head. "Andrew is a good lad. He only needed to be reminded of the truth."

His gaze devoured her face as though he couldn't get enough of her. It was like receiving someone back from the grave, for they had all assumed by now that Brianna was dead.

There was a knock on the door and Sir Bolson opened it. He

frowned at the sight of Brianna locked in Garek's embrace. "Brianna. I thought I would see if there was anything I could do for you."

Brianna extricated herself from Garek's arms and moved out of his reach. "Thank you, Sir Bolson, but there is nothing."

His look passed from one to the other. "There are things I need to discuss with you. I have a message for you from King William himself."

Surprised, Brianna motioned him into the room. "Please, enter. Sir Garek was just leaving."

Garek's eyes flew to hers. She had no right to give him orders and she knew it. And he certainly had no intention of leaving Bolson and Brianna alone.

Her pleading look changed his mind. Her eyes reminded him of his duty, and hers. Anger still rising, he went quickly to the door. "I will see you later."

After the door had closed behind Garek, Bolson crossed to where she sat upon the bench. He looked down at her for a long time. "You are well, Brianna?" he finally asked.

She smiled up at him reassuringly, though there were tears in her eyes. "I am well."

He sat next to Brianna but couldn't bring himself to look at her. Bewildered by his reticence, Brianna prompted him, "What is this message from King William, and how did he come to know about me?"

Taking a deep breath, Sir Bolson lifted his eyes to her face. "His majesty found out about you through me. I knew that this fief was Garek's to hold for William. In actuality, it is William's land."

He stopped and she frowned. "But what has this to do with me?"

Brianna could see him swallow convulsively. "I asked King William to give you to me in marriage."

Brianna's mouth dropped open. "Marriage?! But, Sir Bolson. . ."

"Etienne," he interrupted.

"What?"

"My name is Etienne. I would prefer you use it."

She looked as though she were about to refuse, but then she thought better of it.

"Etienne, why ever would you ask the king if you could marry me? I have no home. I am only a servant in this great hall. Why, I have nothing I can even call my own."

Etienne took her hand in his. "I care not. I wish with all my heart for you to marry me."

Confused, Brianna pulled her hand from his clasp and rose from the bench. She began to pace the room.

"This makes no sense." Stopping, she glared at him. "And what of Mary?"

"Mary has nothing to do with this. This is between you and me."

Brianna was already shaking her head. "Does Garek know of this?"

"He knows."

"And he has agreed?" Brianna was more than a little surprised.

Etienne hesitated so long, Brianna had her answer. She came back and sat beside him again.

"I think you better explain," she told him quietly.

For the first time in a long while, Etienne felt like a child. His tongue tripped over the words he wanted to say.

Brianna faced him solemnly. "You don't love me, Etienne. Why marriage?"

He felt his frustration begin to mount. Taking both of her hands into his, he willed her to understand. "You are so kind and gentle—a bright light in a dark universe. I want to preserve that light."

Her brows drew together. "I do not understand."

"You love Garek. As innocent as you are, that makes you vulnerable." He stared at her intensely. "His darkness will swallow your light. I do not wish to see that happen."

Touched by his chivalry, Brianna pulled one hand free and brushed his face gently with her fingers. Her heart was warmed by his friendship.

"I am honored," she told him softly. "But I cannot marry you."

His face fell, and he turned away. "Then you will remain with Garek, and eventually, he will steal your innocence."

Angered by his assumption that she had no will of her own, she took his chin firmly in her fingers and turned his face back to hers. Her blue eyes became a dark sapphire. "I would not do that. Not to Garek. Not to Marie. And certainly not to my Lord."

Etienne wasn't so sure. It was easy to be firm when temptation was so far away.

"King William has already decided. When he arrives in a few days for Garek's wedding, he will announce ours as well."

Brianna watched him, strangely calm. "We shall see."

❧

Marie wrung out the wet rag and handed it to Brianna. Brianna took it and placed it on the woman's forehead.

"How fare you today, Anne?"

Anne stared back at her from a thin face with sunken eyes. "You should not be here, Brianna," she croaked through dry, cracked lips. "Take Matilda and leave. I am dead already."

"Shhh. Do not speak like that. You will frighten little Matilda."

The young girl in question stared at Brianna with remarkably intelligent eyes for a child of six. "Is my mother going to die, Brianna?"

Brianna wouldn't lie. "We hope not, Matilda. Why don't you go with Marie and tell Alfred that your mother needs some of the white liquid he uses to make breathing easier?"

The child's eyes went from Brianna to her mother. Reluctantly, she allowed Marie to take her from the room.

Anne smiled her thanks. "She is too young to see so much death. First her father. . .now me."

Brianna pushed the straggly hair back from Anne's forehead. She knew the woman hadn't long to live. Already her breathing took on the rattle that was a precursor of death.

A coughing fit brought blood-flecked spittle to her mouth. Brianna gently wiped it away with a soft rag.

"Please. . .please take care of. . .my Matilda," she rasped.

"I will see that she is cared for, Anne. You have my word."

Satisfied, the woman leaned back with a sigh. When Marie and Matilda returned a short time later, Anne was dead.

Brianna and Marie took Matilda with them to the castle. The child clung to Marie, her huge round eyes staring vacantly around her.

Brianna felt for the child. To lose two parents within such a short time would be hard for most adults to bear; how much more so for a child.

"If you think it will be all right, I will keep Matilda with me," Marie told Brianna.

Nodding, Brianna watched the two walk away together, the child's hand firmly clasped within the young woman's. Brianna smiled. Marie would make a fine mother. She often could be seen talking to the children from around the castle. It appeared she had a great love for them.

And she had a talent for dealing with the sick and injured, too. Sir Hormis was evidence of that. When Brianna returned to the castle from the convent, she found the young knight on his feet. Though still a bit pale, his lively personality was quickly returning.

Such thoughts brought more recent reflections to mind. Brianna had made it clear to Garek that she did not relish the attention he lavished upon her. As long as he belonged to Marie, Brianna would not even contemplate a relationship with him.

Etienne, on the other hand, took great pleasure in trying to convince Brianna that she would be happy as his wife. If not for the fact that it would be the first place they would look, she would have fled back to the safety of the convent.

Word arrived by courier that King William would join them on the morrow. Brianna had every intention of asking the king if she might be allowed to finish her vows and become a Benedictine nun. She knew without a doubt that there would never be another man for her. She loved Garek with her entire being, and if they could not be together, she would serve God the rest of her days. Where she had been hesitant before, she now was filled with certainty.

She was just about to douse the torch in her bed chamber when a knock sounded on the door. Thinking it to be Marie, she opened the door without a thought.

Garek faced her across the threshold, his face carefully devoid of emotion. "I would speak with you a moment."

"Aye, milord," she told him, stepping aside so that he might enter. He stayed where he was.

It was then that she noticed he held something carefully within the cupped palms of his hands. He held it out to her and Brianna peered down, seeing a squirming little mass of black.

"I know that Loup cannot be replaced in your affections," he told her. "But I thought perhaps you might consider loving this pup just a little."

Brianna's heart melted at the sight of the wiggling little creature. His tiny eyes had yet to open, just like Loup's in the beginning.

Reaching out, she carefully lifted the pup into her own hands and began cooing softly to it. She turned puzzled eyes up to Garek. "Where is the mother? He is too young to be taken from her yet."

"She was killed by a wild boar. She and all her pups, save this one."

Filled with compassion, Brianna smiled at Garek sadly. "I will try, Garek."

Garek reached out a hand, stroking a finger down her cheek. "If anyone can save him, you can," he told her huskily.

They stared at each other a long moment before Garek turned on his heels and strode away.

≈

Marie sat beside Brianna near the fire, working on her needlework. Little Matilda sat at her side, and the young woman was patiently showing the child how to form the stitches.

Matilda was a bright child, and eager to please. She mimicked Marie in every way possible. Watching the two of them together, one would never know they were not mother and child.

Matilda's hair was very similar in color to Marie's, strengthening the illusion.

Finally, Marie sent the child outside to play. It said something for their growing relationship that the child quickly obeyed, for before she could not be coaxed from the young woman's side.

It had been two months since Matilda joined the castle household. Lammas, the autumn time, was nearing an end and Michaelmas was fast approaching. Already the villagers were preparing for winter.

Word had come from William that his journey to Castle Fenlac would be postponed since the English had again taken to arms and he would be marching forth to crush the rebellion. It was therefore decided that the wedding would be held at Christmas instead.

It seemed everyone breathed a little easier after the news arrived. Still, it was like having the sword of Damocles hanging over one's head.

Marie continued with her tapestry after the child went outside. Brianna could tell that something was on her mind. She waited patiently until the young woman finally looked up, biting her bottom lip.

"Brianna, do you think Garek will allow me to. . .to keep

Matilda after. . .after we are wed?"

Although Garek seemed to like the child, there was no telling what his thoughts were on such a matter. "I honestly cannot say."

Marie continued to chew on her lip. "I have grown to love the child much. I would not wish to lose her."

Brianna smiled. "You have been good for her."

"It is because we understand each other. She lost her mother. . .I lost my father."

"In God's holy Word He tells us that we often suffer so that we can comfort others the same way the Lord comforts us."

"Perhaps that is true, but why must we suffer at all?"

Brianna knew where this conversation was headed. She had heard it often before. "Marie, God did not force Eve to sin. She chose to do so. Her action allowed sin to enter the world."

"And why must we pay for her sin?"

"Why did God's Son have to pay for ours? He did not ask to die. He offered to."

Brianna and Marie continued to talk until Brianna noticed the light growing dim. Hurriedly, she excused herself and went to help Mary in the kitchen.

❧

September twenty-nine arrived and with it the rents due the manor. Mary and Brianna were busy preparing roast goose for the Michaelmas celebration.

As the tenants brought their provender, it was stored in the cellar below the keep and in storehouses built for that purpose. Although the fare was meager, there was still plenty to supply the lord's needs and those of the villeins.

The building of the stone fortress went forward with incredible speed. Every man, woman, and child worked in one capacity or another. They were tireless in their desire to see the land secure.

Brianna watched the building of the castle chapel with satisfaction. Although the main keep would eventually be torn down and rebuilt of stone, Garek chose to build each new building of stone right from the start.

Brianna had been surprised that the previous lord had not built a chapel. It seems he had not been a pious man, though Brianna already knew that was so from the cruelties he had inflicted upon the people.

Garek could be seen everywhere, managing and advising. His knowledge of warfare helped him construct a castle that would repel invaders. For the time being, he kept his distance from Brianna and so did Sir Bolson, but she knew that both men were biding their time until William arrived. They seemed to watch her constantly.

The puppy Garek had given her had survived and was growing, and although he looked nothing like Loup, Brianna treasured him. She had named him Beowulf, and Garek had grinned when she had told him the illustrious story, for it seemed little Beowulf had conquered this castle as easily as his legendary namesake.

Matilda adored the pup and often spent time with him. But although the pup cherished the attention, he would not stray far from Brianna's side.

"That pup reminds me of Sir Bolson," Mary commented one day. "Neither one wanders far when you are near."

Brianna sighed. "Mary."

"Nay, Brianna. It is fine. You tried to warn me often enough but I would not listen. I tried to make the knight dance to my tune, but he was not so easily made to do so."

"Are you grieved over it?"

Mary watched from the door to the cooking chamber as Sir Bolson practiced his swordplay in the distance. "I am not certain."

Brianna hugged her friend. "There is still time. Sir Bolson does not love me."

Mary shook her head sadly. "Perhaps not, but neither does he love me."

Not knowing what to say, Brianna took refuge in silence. Both women silently finished preparing the feast for Michaelmas in honor of Saint Michael, the archangel, patron saint of knights.

❧

November, the blood month, came and the villeins were busy slaughtering animals for winter sustenance. Brianna shivered at the thought of the killing, but she well knew the arts of preservation.

She handed Mary another salt block, and Mary began to crush it with the pestle in the mortar bowl.

Taking slices of meat, Brianna added them to the brine barrel, making sure the meat was covered with the salt solution. Although the meat would have to be soaked prior to cooking to remove most of the brine, still the salt gave it extra flavor.

While Brianna finished the meat, Mary helped the other kitchen maids as they prepared the barrels of mustard. Everyone was busy with some chore. Even Garek was helping with the slaughter.

Brianna could see Garek outside, his broad, muscled shape standing out among the smaller villeins. Everywhere Garek went, his vital presence seemed to give life to the atmosphere.

Brianna always knew when Garek was close. Often he would catch her eye and she would find it hard to look away. His gray eyes spoke volumes to her.

As Saint Nicholas' Day approached, tempers began to flare. Time was growing short, and the precariousness of their situation was unsettling. Often Garek and Etienne could be found in heated discussion.

Brianna began to lose weight, and though she was thin to begin with, she started to take on an emaciated appearance. Etienne was the first to comment upon it. He cornered her in the chapel where she often went to pray, even though the building was as yet unfinished. He waited until she had concluded her prayers before sitting on the bench beside her. He didn't look at her, but instead studied the cross on the wall in front of them.

"I came to tell you that when King William arrives, I will not force you to marry me." He turned to look at her then and she stared steadily back at him. She waited without speaking for him to continue.

"You look like a walking skeleton, and I am afraid much of this is because of me. You need fear me no longer. I want you to know, though, that if you change your mind, I will still be here for you."

Brianna knew he was trying to ease her mind, but more than the thought of marrying him plagued her. Still, it was a relief to know Etienne would consider her feelings above his own.

She wasn't sure how to answer him, so she reverted to teasing. "You were worried that Saint Nicholas would not leave you any gifts."

He gave her a halfhearted grin. "There is only one gift I truly want," he told her softly.

"You think so now, but sometimes the wanting is more desirable than the having."

He got slowly to his feet. "If you need me, will you call on me?"

She took his hand in hers. Her heart was full to overflowing with love for him. Why couldn't she love him differently? Was it possible she could learn to love him the same way she loved Garek? No. She knew she could not, and anything less for someone like Etienne was unthinkable. He deserved the best God had to give him.

"I will."

"Do I have your word on it?"

She smiled, the teasing glint back in her eyes. "You may be sorry one day that you offered."

He grinned back at her, shaking his head, and turning, left her sitting alone with her thoughts.

# twelve

Brianna deftly twisted dry grape vines into a huge wreath. At the top she tied one end of a long ivy vine, winding it around the grape vines until the whole wreath was covered in green.

Matilda handed her sprigs of holly berries that she tied intermingled with the leaves.

The little girl smiled at Brianna. "You do that well, Brianna. It is beautiful." She sighed. "I wish I could do that. It looks like more fun than sewing."

Brianna hid a grin. Little Matilda didn't take well to being a lady. She had been much too used to running free in the great outdoors, and sitting endless hours while she tried to perfect tiny little stitches was not what she considered fun. Yet she tried hard, because she wanted to please Marie.

"Would you like to try?" Brianna asked her.

Her eyes lit up and she vigorously nodded her head. Taking some of the dried vines, Brianna handed them to the child and proceeded to show her how to twist them into wreaths. The final outcome was not perfect but it was very good for a first try. Brianna praised her efforts and was rewarded with a huge smile.

Christmas was a very important holiday for the people of the manor. The villeins looked forward to having a fortnight free from labor, from Christmas Eve until Twelfth Night.

Already the fields had been cleared by the cattle and were barren of everything, even stubble. After Twelfth Night, it would be time to ready the fields for planting.

Mary was busy in the kitchen with some of the other women, making candles that Garek intended to use as gifts to the villeins. It was a luxury that would be very appreciated.

Several of the villeins had been sent into the forest to clear it of dead wood and to choose a few other trees that would be used for firewood for the manor's servants. The firewood would be a generous bonus gift from the lord of the manor.

Everywhere the servants were bustling in preparation for the coming holiday and the arrival of the king.

Brianna took the wreath she had finished and called for Gavin, the manor chamberlain. Together they managed to hoist the monstrous wreath to the center of the wall above the dais at the far end of the room. Gavin dropped the wreath onto the peg protruding from the wall.

Satisfied, Brianna went back to help Matilda with her own wreath. In the end it was decided that Matilda could use the decoration for her and Marie's room. Marie had generously allowed the child to sleep with her, together sharing the same bed.

After helping the girl hang the wreath in the bed chamber, Brianna returned to finish decorating the main hall. She hung kissing balls from the ceiling rafters, the clean scent of bay and cloves adding a pungent scent to the smoky room.

Gavin had opened the windows, but still much smoke from the fire hung suspended in the great room, for there was nowhere for it to go but out the small windows and the main door when it was opened. One grew accustomed to the smoky atmosphere.

Everywhere the hall was decked with red and green, increasing the festivity. Green was the symbol of continued life throughout the winter, and red the symbol of Christ's blood. Brianna took this seasonal opportunity to explain the symbolism to anyone and everyone who would listen. Many, whether touched by the season or not, gave their lives to Christ.

Smiling at Sir Triden as he passed her on his way to see Garek, Brianna realized for the first time how much she missed seeing most of Garek's knights around the manor, for Garek had given each man his own fief and they were busily preparing their own homes.

Serin and Aleene would be coming for the Christmas celebration, and Brianna could hardly wait to see them. Aleene
was already heavy with child, and it looked like she might be
the first to produce offspring in the coming year.

That she and Serin were happy was obvious, and it gave
Brianna great pleasure to watch their loving interchanges. If
she grew melancholy over the thought that she could not share
the same joy, she firmly berated herself for such thoughts.

Although special rents were due from the tenants at
Christmastide, Garek had chosen to suspend them and allow
the tenants to keep what little provender they had. Since the
country was still recovering from the ravages of war, it was a
generous offer and was greatly appreciated.

Whether it was his intention or no, Garek was amassing a
devoted band of followers. Even young Andrew, the villein
who had visited Brianna at the convent, had succumbed to his
benevolence.

Such things only made Brianna's own love for the man
grow stronger. She could see how God was using Garek to
serve her people, for a different lord might not have been so
kind. She truly believed that God had a purpose for his life.

For the most part, Garek left Brianna alone. But there were
times when they would be accidentally thrown together and
Brianna would have to fight the attraction she felt for him.

It was only two days until Christmas and Brianna was
busily arranging tablecloths on the extra trestle tables in
preparation for King William's arrival the next day. Rain
poured from leaden skies, leaving the manor house dank and
cold. The torches could not dispel the gloom, and Brianna
shivered with the clammy cold.

Garek strode into the room, stopping just over the threshold. He hadn't realized that Brianna was in the room, and
even now he felt a thrill run through him at the sight of her.
His eyes skimmed her figure, noticing that although she had

managed to regain some weight, she was still little more than bones.

Dark circles under her eyes spoke of sleepless nights. He empathized with her, for his own nights were much the same. He knew this came from worrying over the future, but he wondered how much was due to their close proximity to each other.

Still, until he could speak with William, there was nothing he could do.

Brianna stood, pulling the table linen to her chest. "I. . .I was preparing the room for the morrow," she told him, realizing they were alone.

He continued to stare at her and Brianna noticed the tick in his cheek. She saw him take a deep breath and then walk to the fire, bending down and reaching his frozen fingers toward the warmth. "It is no matter. Finish what you are doing."

Brianna chanced a glance at him and noticed his condition. His hair clung wetly to his head as his clothes did to his body. His tunic was shredded and hung in strips. Brianna's eyes went wide.

"What happened?"

Garek pulled the torn garment over his head, twisted it into a ball, and threw it into the fire. He rose to his feet intending to retrieve a fresh tunic, when Brianna noticed the lacerations across his arms and chest.

"Garek! You are hurt."

Dumping the linen on the floor, she crossed quickly to him. She gently stroked a finger across a bloody welt, and as she did, Garek pulled away from her. "It is nothing."

Hands planted firmly on her hips, Brianna glared at him. "It is something. If the wounds are not tended, they may fester and poison your blood. Stay just as you are and I will fetch a healing balm that Alfred left for me."

"Brianna. . ."

One look from those fierce blue eyes silenced him. Shrugging, he returned to his place by the fire, leaning forward to absorb more of the meager heat.

Brianna was back in a moment, carrying a basket with linen strips and the concoction she had spoken of. She came and stood between his knees and gently began to rub the salve into his wounds. So fierce was her concentration, she failed to notice the darkening of the gray eyes before her.

"How did this happen?"

Garek sucked in a sharp breath as the salve began to sting the wounds. "We were cutting the tree for the Yule log. One of the villeins, Matthew I think his name was, did not see the tree falling in his direction."

She looked into his eyes, her own softening. "You saved him?" It was more a statement than a question.

"I merely shoved him out of the way."

She frowned. "But how did you come by these cuts?"

One corner of his mouth turned up in a half grin. "The tree fell on me instead," he told her sheepishly.

Her face paled, and Garek noticed. "It is nothing, I tell you. I am well, though minus one tunic."

Taking a deep breath she tried to match his light tone. "I will make you another."

He grinned at her, and she smiled in return. She took another dip of salve but Garek took her gently by the wrist when she reached toward his chest to apply it. "It is enough," he told her, an odd note in his voice.

She glanced at him in surprise, her brows furrowed in consternation. "But I am not finished."

Garek chose his words carefully. "Brianna, if you do not leave this room now, you might not leave it at all."

Her eyes jerked up to his and for the first time she noticed the desire therein. She swallowed hard, a rosy hue staining her cheeks. Again it occurred to her how very alone they were.

Slowly he released her wrist and she hastily smoothed the salve back into its container. "As you wish, milord," she answered breathlessly. "I will leave the salve for you to apply."

Quickly gathering up the basket and the linen, Brianna made a hasty exit, her heart thundering in her chest.

Garek watched her leave, his face devoid of emotion. Sighing loudly, he leaned his head in his hands, tiredly rubbing his face. He could feel his heart slow from its erratic pace. Something had to be done. And soon.

❧

Brianna wasn't sure what she had expected, but this certainly was not it. King William was tall and well built, his face clean shaven in the Norman style. His reddish hair cupped closely around his head like a cap and he had a firm, angular jaw. The jaw itself told her he was a man to be reckoned with.

It still amazed her that a man from such humble beginnings had risen to such great power despite being an illegitimate son. Still, there was something about the merry twinkle in his brown eyes that assured Brianna the man was not quite as ruthless as others suggested. Fortunately for Brianna, she had no knowledge of his martial exploits, or she would not have felt so secure in her assessment of the conqueror.

William greeted Garek as though they were old friends. When he climbed from his mount he stood shorter than the dark knight by several inches, but he was still a commanding figure.

William seemed to know all of Garek's knights and it was obvious they held him in high esteem. They had all arrived only that morning to pay their respects to their king.

It was Etienne who took Brianna by the hand and pulled her forward to meet the king. Brianna did not miss the lowering of Garek's angry brows. Curtsying low before William, Brianna found the king's unsmiling gaze focused upon her. She wondered what the knight had told his king.

"So, this is the blue-eyed angel."

Brianna flushed a becoming red. "Sire, I think you have been misinformed."

"Perhaps," he agreed. "We shall see."

They made their way into the great hall of the keep and William looked around in appreciation of the structure.

"Chevier did well for himself. Is this how you found it?"

Garek nodded. "Aye, Sire. We have made a few changes and additions, but for the most part, this is what it looked like when I arrived."

William shook his head sadly. "Poor Chevier." His looked roamed the room. "Where is Marie Waverly? I would offer my condolences."

"She is attending to some things," Brianna answered him. "She did not know you had arrived or she would have been here to meet you."

William's gaze focused on Brianna again. "We have many things to discuss, Garek, but for now I could use a drink."

"What would you have, my liege? We can offer you ale, wine, even water or milk."

The king grinned. "I will save that pleasure for my later years, if I have any. Have you any mulled wine?"

"Certainly." Garek motioned to the butler who brought the king a tankard of the steaming brew, then he hastened to the buttery to retrieve a few extra bottles of wine to be mulled.

Garek gave his own great chair to William, then the others of the king's party made themselves comfortable around the circular fire hearth.

The tree Garek had chopped the previous day now was displayed prominently, taking up the whole hearth. It would continue to burn until Twelfth Night.

Brianna tried not to look at the huge log because every time she did, she remembered yesterday. She glanced at Garek and found him watching her, a knowing smile upon his lips. Coloring hotly, Brianna excused herself to the kitchen.

Since it was nearly time for the evening meal, the hall servants were in the process of setting up the trestle tables. The laundress sighed as she watched the table cloths being draped, for it meant extra work for her now that there were twice as many people to feed. Brianna smiled sympathetically.

Mary, on the other hand, thrived on the extra work. Either that, or one of the king's knights who had traveled with William had caught her interest. Her eyes sparkled, and her face was flushed.

Brianna shook her head, one corner of her mouth twisting wryly. She hoped her friend would one day settle down. But although Mary was long past earliest marrying age, her beauty guaranteed she would not have to remain that way. Of course, beauty was fleeting, as King Solomon had said. Brianna fervently hoped her friend would choose to marry soon.

When Brianna returned to the great hall, she found Garek and William deep in conversation. Periodically their laughter reached her ears and she wondered what they were discussing.

Since Marie Waverly had not yet made an appearance, Brianna went in search of her. She found her in the chapel, on her knees. Surprised, Brianna waited until the young woman rose to her feet before making any movement.

Marie glanced up and saw Brianna at the door. She smiled hesitantly as she approached her. "I have thought a lot about what you have told me, and I have decided to give my life to Christ. I came here to tell Him that I trust Him, and that I will abide by His will for my life, whether that be as lady of this manor or not."

Tears came to Brianna's eyes, and reaching out, she hugged Marie. "I am so glad for you. And remember, He will always be here for you. You can turn every burden over to Him and let Him do the worrying for you."

Marie studied her friend quietly. "If you believe that to be true, Brianna, then why do you look like you do? Why are there circles under your eyes and your clothes hanging from you like sacks?"

Brianna could only stare. Marie shrugged her shoulders. "You were looking for me?"

Pulling herself from the daze that Marie's words had sent

her into, Brianna nodded. "Yea. King William has arrived and would like to see you."

Although the color left the younger woman's face, the peaceful serenity of her eyes never wavered. "I will go see him now."

When Brianna didn't follow her, Marie turned in surprise. "Are you not coming with me?"

"Nay. I will come soon, but I wish to spend some time here first."

A brief smile of understanding touched the other girl's lips. "I will tell Garek."

Brianna didn't hear her. Indeed, Brianna's thoughts were on what Marie had said earlier. Going to the forward bench, Brianna seated herself, her eyes fixed upward on the wooden cross that been carved by the village carpenter. She knew Dressler would be happy with all the business the manor was giving him, but of all his work, this carving was by far the best she had ever seen.

She stared intently at the cross, her mind churning with her thoughts.

Marie had accepted Christ and had immediately rested on His promises to provide what was necessary for her life. She trusted God, so no matter what might come, Marie knew all things would work out for her own good. She trusted God. She trusted God! The words seemed to echo in Brianna's mind.

Brianna hung her head in shame. For all her mouthing of platitudes and admonishments to others, she knew she had not trusted the Lord with her own life lately. She had been fretting and fussing, begging and pleading, never trusting that God knew what He was about.

"Forgive me, Lord," she whispered. "Help me to trust in You and never forget that whatever happens, nothing happens that is not according to Your will."

She felt a sense of peace, which had been missing from her life lately, begin to flow through her again. It was only when her eyes turned outward that she was drawn away from God's will for her life. This was the time she was weakest, and Satan realized this and attacked her vulnerability. When her eyes were turned inward, then and only then was she focused on God's will for her life.

She felt movement at her feet and looked down. "What are you doing here? How did you get out of our room?"

Beowulf's little black tail wagged rapidly against the stone floor. Black beady eyes sparkled up at her from a bewhiskered face that surrounded a perpetual grin.

"He was lonely."

Brianna whirled around to face little Matilda. Brianna smiled in sympathy. So much had been happening the last few days to get ready for the king's arrival, that neither Marie nor Brianna had had much time for the child. "And were you lonely also?"

Auburn curls bobbing, the child climbed up on the bench next to Brianna. Matilda studied Brianna thoughtfully.

"My mama prayed a lot. So did my daddy. Why are you praying? Does God really listen to you? He did not listen to my mama."

Pruning this tangled comment to its essence took but a moment, and Brianna cut to the heart of the child's concern. "Why do you think God did not listen to your mama?"

Matilda shrugged, pursing her lips and turning to the cross. "She asked Him to keep my daddy safe, but he died anyway. She also asked Him to make her well, but she. . .she still died."

Brianna took the child onto her lap. "Then He still answered her, Matilda."

Surprised, the girl turned to inspect Brianna's face curiously. "He did?"

Brianna nodded her head. "Yea, Matilda. He always answers our prayers." She hesitated a moment and then told the child softly, "He said, Nay."

It took a moment for the words to sink in. The wonder on the child's face brought a small smile to Brianna's. "You mean that God says nay just like mama and papa did sometimes?"

Brianna nodded. "Sometimes we do not understand why, but God does. We just have to trust Him."

Looking as though she had been caught stealing, Matilda ducked her head. "I heard you talking to God. I heard you say that you would trust Him. I am sorry that I listened."

Brianna hugged the child close. "I do not mind. Would you like to pray with me?"

Looking unsure of herself, the child nodded nonetheless. Brianna took Matilda's small hand into her own and they bowed their heads together while Beowulf, still grinning, looked on.

❧

Garek watched William as he rose to greet Marie Waverly. He looked truly pleased to see her, and lifting the woman from her deep curtsy, he turned a still-smiling face to Garek.

"She is as beautiful as ever, do you not agree, Garek?"

Garek's scrutiny passed quickly over the girl. She was indeed beautiful. "Aye, Sire."

The smile left William's face. "I am sorry about your father, my dear. I wish I could have prevented it."

"Thank you, Sire. He. . .he always appreciated your friendship."

"As I did his. I could not have so easily conquered this fair land if not for friends like him." William's smile returned. "And tomorrow will see you settled in this manor as the lady that you are."

Marie exchanged glances with Garek, before dropping her eyes. "As you wish, milord."

"Have you aught to say on the matter?" the king asked, touching her face gently with his cupped hand and lifting it for his inspection.

For a moment Marie was tempted to tell this mighty man

just what she thought of this arranged marriage. But only for a moment. Her father's image passed before her eyes and she remembered her promise to him.

"Nay, milord. There is nothing."

## thirteen

Brianna sat beside Marie as the young woman worked patiently at her tapestry. The needle moved smoothly in and out, and so intense was her concentration that Brianna was startled when she spoke.

"Brianna, if it were possible, would you marry Garek?"

Marie didn't look up from her sewing, missing Brianna's panicked expression.

"Why would you ask such a thing?"

This time, the girl did look up, her eyes fixed on Brianna's wary blue ones. "You love him, and he you."

About to deny it, Marie waved her hand in the air. "I am not a fool, Brianna, though some might think otherwise. Is it me that keeps you apart?"

Brianna rose to her feet. "Let us not discuss it. The matter is settled."

Marie sighed. "You are my friend, Brianna, and I would do anything in my power to see you as happy as you deserve to be. If only I had not made such a promise to my father."

"What promise?"

Marie turned away. She put down her sewing, and getting to her feet wandered over to the window. Leaning upon the sill, she pushed open the shutters, allowing chill, wet air to enter the hall.

Brianna could see by her look that Marie's thoughts were far away, and from the direction of her gaze, it didn't take much to guess what was on her mind. Crossing to her side, Brianna put an arm around Marie's waist and studied the dirt mound on the hill in the distance.

Marie's voice was little more than a sigh. "I gave him my

solemn oath that I would wed according to King William's decree. My father only wanted to return to the England he loved and to have back a portion of the land that was taken from him. But he also wanted to assure a home for me in Normandy if something should happen to him here."

Brianna took a deep breath. "It would seem there were a lot of oaths taken without thought to the consequences."

Dropping her head, Marie only nodded.

"I must see about preparing things for the morrow." Giving Marie a last sympathetic look, Brianna started to leave, but Marie's voice stopped her.

"I have a secret that I wish to share with you."

Feeling uncomfortable, Brianna hesitated. She wasn't sure she wanted to hear what the younger woman had to say. "If it is a secret—"

"It is only a secret to myself. I wanted to tell you so that you know I understand about you and Garek." Marie turned from the window and looked Brianna in the eye. "I am in love with someone, and he is in love with me. He has told me. But I gave my oath to King William and my father, and also to Garek. I will not break my oath."

Brianna stared at her in surprise. Her head began to swim with possibilities, but she firmly reined in her wayward thoughts. This really changed nothing. King William was bent on seeing this marriage through.

"I am sorry," she answered softly.

She could barely hear Marie's muttered words as she left the hall. "For all of us."

෴

Brianna left the kitchen after making arrangements for the next day. More help had been enlisted of the villeins in the village who had suddenly become eager in their desire for festivities.

She descended the stone steps and headed for the chapel where she spent much of her time lately. Marie's challenge to her faith had caused Brianna to do some soul searching, and she had spent much time in prayer. As a result, Brianna had found the peace she had been missing.

Pale light shone from the arched windows, reminding Brianna of Garek's command that the candles in the chapel be constantly lit from sundown until sunrise. The door stood before her, massive and solid, the iron studs reflecting the bright moonlight. She pushed open the door and went inside.

She was halfway down the aisle to the altar when she realized she wasn't alone. Sucking in a breath, she stopped suddenly, one hand to her racing heart. A figure rose from the bench before the altar and she recognized Garek's tall form.

"Milord, you frightened me," she told him breathlessly. She watched him apprehensively. "I can come back another time."

She turned to leave, but he was beside her in an instant. "Do not go. I was awaiting you." He tried to take her hand but she put them behind her back, clasping them together.

Garek sighed. "Brianna, there are things that I must say to you, and tonight is the only time that I may. Tomorrow—"

"Tomorrow you will be wed," she finished for him, her voice tight. "There is nothing good that can be said this night."

Curling his large hand around her arm, he pulled her forward until she was beside the front bench. He pushed her gently into the seat. "Please, listen."

He seated himself beside her but didn't touch her. His eyes focused on the carved wooden cross over the altar.

"When you were gone, I thought you might be. . .dead," he finished softly. "I decided there was nothing for me to lose, so I prayed to God."

Startled, Brianna's interest quickened, but she remained silent.

"I told Him that if He would bring you back to me, I would treat you more honorably in the future." His eyes came back to roam her face, tracing her features as though to commit them firmly to memory. "He answered my prayer, and I will keep my promise."

He reached out to touch her but stopped just short of her cheek. Slowly he dropped his hand to his side, curling his fingers into a ball. He turned back to the cross.

"I will renounce my vow to William. I will take you as my wife."

Brianna felt a little thrill at his words. She was touched that Garek cared enough to forsake his honor, and his king, just for her but she knew she could never let him do it.

Careful not to touch him, she leaned close to make her words ring clear. "In the Holy Scriptures there is much mentioned of vows. It has been made clear that vows should not be entered into lightly. King Solomon himself is believed to have said that when you make a vow to God, you should not delay in fulfilling it. God has no pleasure in fools; you should fulfill your vow. He said that it is better not to make a vow than to make a vow and not fulfill it." Hesitantly she lay her hand upon his. As she expected, she could feel the heat course through her body. Garek's eyes when he turned to face her told her he was experiencing the same thing.

"I cannot vow to love Marie Waverly when I love you with every fiber of my being. There will never be anyone else for me."

Brianna dropped her hand and turned away. "In time—"

"Nay!" he interrupted. "Time will not matter. I will love you until the day that I die. God willing, that will be soon, for I cannot long bear this pain."

Breathing in sharply, Brianna turned to him in anger. "You must never say such a thing. Your life is a gift from God."

At his grunt of denial, she took him firmly by the jaw and turned him back to face her. Garek was suddenly mesmerized by the dark, glittering depths of sapphire eyes sparkling with anger. When she had his attention, Brianna released him.

"All God has ever wanted from you, Garek, is to be allowed

to be your Father. He wants to give you the desires of your heart, but instead He will give you what you need. Ask what you will, and if it is in accord with His will for you, He will grant it."

"I want you."

Brianna felt her heart begin to thump erratically at the passionate declaration. Dear God, why? Why did this have to happen? What was the purpose?

Brianna tried again. "Garek, your life is a gift from God. What you do with that life is your gift to Him. Until you can accept that—asking forgiveness of your sins and being willing to be His child—you will never be the man God intended you to be."

"Will He then give you to me?"

Sighing, Brianna turned away. "You must do this for yourself, not for me."

"I have lived in the darkness so long, I do not think I can live in the light, as you do."

"You must try," she said, rising to her feet. "Talk to Him, Garek. Listen with your heart, for I know you have one. The prophet Jeremiah said, 'I have not lost sight of my plan for you, the Lord says, and it is your welfare I have in mind, not your undoing; for you, too, I have a destiny and a hope. Cry out to me then, and your suit will prosper; plead with me, and I will listen; look for me, and you shall find me, if you look for me in good earnest. Find me you shall, the Lord says, and your sentence of exile shall be reversed.' "

The power of the holy words could be heard in the resonance of Brianna's voice. Garek felt chills raise the skin on his forearms, and he hungered to believe what she said.

Brianna looked him steadily in the eye. "You are a captive of sin, Garek, an exile from God. Let Him free you as He wants to so that you can be united with Him. Believe on His Son and trust in His salvation."

Garek watched her walk up the aisle and out the door. He

laid his head upon his forearms, draped over the railing
before him. Such overwhelming pain and loss filled his being
that he began to quietly sob. Lifting his head to the cross, the
candlelight reflected from the tears on his face.

"Dear God," he begged, "forgive me." Dropping his head
back to his arms, his voice sounded in the chapel, hollow
with despair. "Forgive me."

❧

Christmas morning dawned with overcast skies portending
more rain and cold. Marie shivered as she watched Brianna
tend the fire in the main hall.

"It is an evil omen," she told Brianna. "No good can come
of this day."

"Marie," Brianna admonished. "You know that there are no
such things as evil omens. Nothing happens that is not
according to God's will. Remember that."

Marie jumped to her feet. "How can this be God's will?"
she cried in anguish. "How?" She turned her eyes upward.
"Merciful God, how can You let this happen? What is it You
want from me?"

Seeing the young woman growing more distraught,
Brianna hastened to reassure her and turn her mind to other
things.

"Will you go hunting with the king this morning?"

Marie shook her head. "Nay. I am not in the mood for
sport, much less such a barbarous one."

King William entered the hall ahead of Garek, Etienne, Sir
Hormis, and others intending to go on the hunt. The king was
in a jovial mood, but it didn't take long for him to perceive
that others were not. He was a wise and discerning man, so he
said nothing except to inquire if Marie would join them for
the morning's sport.

The wedding had been set for evening, and it was intended
that the rest of the day be dedicated, not only to the merriment of the event, but to observing Christmas as well.

Garek was dressed in the new raiment the king had given him as a Christmas gift. Garek had done the same for his own knights, and although the band looked jolly in their apparel, many dour faces denied that conclusion.

The king's voice was gentle as he addressed Marie. "My dear, nothing will happen to you with my knights by your side, I promise you."

Realizing he was referring to her father, Marie was moved by his words. In his way, King William really did care for her.

"I beg leave of you, Sire. There is much to be done here."

William grinned. "It is a woman's way, is it not?" He shook his head, his eyes gleaming with merriment. "Weddings and birthings. Nothing seems to mean more to a woman. So be it, child."

Brianna's eyes went to Garek, standing straight and tall beside his king. Lebeau rested on his forearm, reminding Brianna of the first time she had seen him.

When Garek's eyes locked with hers, Brianna frowned. Something was missing, and she couldn't quite put a name to it. He turned away, but Brianna continued to study him, curious about the difference in him. Finally, it dawned on her. The pain was gone from his eyes. There was a tranquillity about Garek that Brianna had never seen before, a softness about his features.

A commotion disrupted Brianna's thoughts as the huntsman entered the hall with the dogs and their handlers.

"We are ready, Sire."

Brianna and Marie watched them from the open door, shivering at the cold bite of the wind.

The alaunts were being used today for the wild boar, instead of the greyhounds used for hunting deer, and the raucous noise they made brought a smile to Brianna's face. She could hear Beowulf returning their call from her upper room, his puppy bark no more than a small yelp.

The sergeants were wisely dressed in furs, their beating

sticks looking lethal in their hands. The whole party mounted up and headed out of the castle, Garek's look sliding over Brianna as he went by.

Brianna and Marie separated to their various duties to begin preparing the great hall for the coming ceremony. Brianna worked with a hollow feeling in the pit of her stomach. Each moment that brought the ceremony closer seemed to send her deeper into a world that seemed surreal. She felt numb.

Hours that normally dragged by seemed to be flying by like speeding arrows.

Marie sought out Brianna, her worried frown bringing Brianna to her feet next to the hearth where she had been preparing blancmange for the evening. She had just added the sugar to the paste of chicken and rice when Marie found her, her agitation evident by the twisting of her linen handkerchief.

"Brianna, have you seen Matilda?"

"Nay, is she missing?"

Marie bit her bottom lip. "We cannot find her. I have searched everywhere, and have others doing the same."

Brianna put down her spoon and untied the rag from around her waist. "I will help you look for her."

Giving instructions to one of the serving girls to watch the food, Brianna followed Marie from the room.

"Let us check with the gatekeeper," Brianna told the younger girl. "Maybe he saw her leave."

The gatekeeper confirmed Brianna's suspicions, but it worried her more when the man informed her that Beowulf had been with the child.

Brianna thought it more than likely that Matilda had been feeling lonesome again, and hearing Beowulf's cries that morning must have decided that he felt the same.

"I will go and look for her," Marie suggested. "You see if you can find someone to help us."

It was early afternoon when the searchers returned to the castle. No one had been able to locate the girl, or the pup.

Only Marie was still out searching, the others having returned to see if there had been any news.

Before long the hunting party returned, their laughter sounding odd against the stillness of the castle. Garek was the first to notice that something was amiss. He glanced around until his gaze fastened on Brianna. Having found her, he relaxed a bit and dismounted.

"What goes on here?"

"Matilda is missing," Brianna informed him. "We have searched everywhere but cannot find her."

Already the knights were remounting. Garek swung himself back into his saddle. "Which direction?"

Brianna showed him, standing by the king as they watched the others ride swiftly out of the castle enclosure.

It seemed an eternity before they returned, tired and discouraged. No one had been able to locate the child. It was as though she had disappeared from the face of the earth. What was more, Marie Waverly was now missing also.

King William's displeasure was evident. "Do you think it might be brigands? Raiders?"

Brianna went cold at the thought. Would they harm a helpless child? What they might do to a woman as beautiful as Marie, was obvious.

"If they have harmed one hair of her head, I will slay every one of them, if my search takes me to the ends of the earth."

Surprised by Sir Hormis's vehement declaration, King William frowned at the young knight. "What say you, Hormis?"

The young knight's face colored crimson, but his look remained fixed steadily on his king. "She has been kind to me. She. . .she helped me to recover after my attack and being left for dead."

Garek was studying the knight thoughtfully. He spoke to William, but his eyes remained fixed on Sir Hormis. "There were three dead bodies near where we found Sir Hormis and Earl Waverly. Sir Hormis did not surrender without a fight."

The king's look returned to contemplate the knight before him. His look wandered around the group surrounding him. "You have my eternal gratitude. I will see what can be done about repaying you later, but right now we need to find Marie and my wife's namesake."

Surprised, it took a moment for Brianna to realize that little Matilda did indeed bear the name of the king's wife.

A knight came quickly into the hall. "We have found them."

Brianna couldn't remember exactly what happened over the next several hours. It seems that Matilda had wandered rather far from the castle, Beowulf happily keeping her company. Then they had gotten too close to the river, and the bank, having been softened by the recent rains, gave way, sending both Matilda and the pup into the freezing water.

Somehow, Beowulf had managed to help keep the child afloat until she could grab a branch from a tree that was drifting in the water. When the branch finally lodged against a jutting log, Matilda clung to both it and the pup until Marie eventually found them. In trying to rescue them, Marie's gunna became tangled in the branches and the rescuer became a prisoner as well.

Now Brianna hustled around trying to get everyone dry and warm, but a castle was not very conducive to this. No matter how hot the fire, the hall never seemed to be warm.

It was some time later, as Brianna handed them each a mug of hot milk, that it occurred to her that the time set for the wedding ceremony had passed. By common consent, it would seem, the wedding was postponed.

Garek found Brianna helping a shivering Marie and Matilda into bed. His look passed over each before returning to Brianna.

"The king wishes to speak with you, Brianna." As she straightened, he glanced at Marie. "And you also, Marie."

"Now?" Brianna asked. "Could it not wait?"

"King William waits for no one," he informed her. "In the great hall."

They watched him walk away, and Marie quickly arose, pulling her soft kirtle over her head. Brianna helped her into her gunna, and after seeing that Matilda was asleep, they quickly made their way to where the king awaited them.

When they entered the room, they found it empty save for the king, Garek, Etienne, and Sir Hormis.

"Come forward," the king commanded, and both women hastened to obey. Dropping into a deep curtsy before him, they awaited his word before rising to their feet.

Sighing, the king leaned back in the chair ordinarily reserved for Garek at mealtimes. "It would seem there are things that need to be attended to," he told them. He looked at Etienne. "Sir Bolson, you have asked for the hand of the maid, Brianna. Is this not so?"

Brianna's eyes flew to Garek. His face was pale, the tick that told of feelings held in check apparent in his cheek. Her look then passed to Etienne, who stood silently watching her.

"Yea, Sire."

The king's gaze fastened on Brianna. "And what have you to say to this?"

"Sire," Brianna began, hating the hurt she knew she would cause the young knight. "I do not love Sir Bolson as he deserves to be loved. I do not believe it is God's will for my life that I do this."

"I have already agreed to this marriage," William told her implacably, but he glanced again at Sir Bolson. "What is your will on this matter?"

Etienne's intense look settled once again on Brianna. "I wish only to make Brianna happy. If she cannot be so with me, then I release her."

Nodding, the king then turned to Garek. "And Sir Garek, the time for your wedding is past. Shall we try again for the morrow?"

Garek swallowed hard. "I will keep my oath."

"And you, Marie?"

Marie dropped her eyes to the floor. "It was the wish of my father that I marry whomever you chose for me, Sire."

William rose and went to her side. He touched her gently on the cheek with the backs of his fingers, cupped her chin, and raised her eyes to his.

"And if I gave you the choice?"

Marie's look flickered briefly to Sir Hormis before her lashes swept down over pale cheeks. "I made a promise to my father."

"Ah. You promised him to marry a landed gentleman with fiefs on both sides of the channel?"

She nodded. "Yea, Sire."

William released her and went to Sir Hormis. "Sir Hormis, I told you that I would reward you for valor in trying to save the life of my dear friend, Earl Waverly. For such a daring act of bravery I feel you should be allowed your own fief in this fair land to add to the one you already own in Normandy. Is this acceptable to you?"

There was a strange glitter in the knight's eyes as they rested on Marie. "Yea, Sire."

Rocking back on his heels, William then crossed his hands over his chest, pursing his lips. "Then Marie Waverly, I am allowing you your choice of husband. Is it Garek du Mor you would have?"

Marie's look flashed to Garek, who stood open-mouthed before his king. "Nay, Sire. If it would so please him, I would choose Sir Hormis."

"And Sir Hormis," the king inquired of his knight. "Would this please you?"

Eyes glinting, Sir Hormis grinned at William. "Aye, Sire. It would please me well."

Brianna's heart gave a leap and her joyous eyes found Garek's. His puzzled look wandered the group around him before the king's and Marie's words finally sank in. Gray eyes came alive with jubilation.

King William was shaking his head sadly, though his brown eyes sparkled. "It would seem, Sir Garek, that you have been rejected. Would you care for me to arrange another match for you?"

Garek's eyes never left Brianna's. "If it would not seem forward, Sire, I would like to arrange my own."

William laughed. "So be it." Suddenly he sobered, turning to Sir Bolson. "And you, Etienne? What of you?"

"If I have your permission, Sire, I should like to return to Normandy."

"We shall miss you in England, but I think I understand. Go with my blessings."

"If it is all the same to you, Sire, I should like to leave at first light."

William nodded, and Etienne turned to leave the room. Brianna quickly followed him to the door. She smiled softly into his sad eyes. "Godspeed," she told him.

He touched her cheek a moment, returning her smile halfway. "Be happy. I will always remember you."

Brianna watched him leave, feeling curiously bereft. She felt Garek's presence behind her.

"Will you come to the chapel with me?"

Nodding, Brianna received permission from the king to leave. She allowed Garek to place her fur mantle around her shoulders and together they descended the stairs to the forecourt. As they circled the manor house, Garek took Brianna's hand firmly into his own.

Opening the door for her, Garek followed Brianna inside. He took her hand again and led her to the front bench, where they had talked only the night before. Had it been only one night? To Garek it seemed an eon had passed since then.

He seated Brianna on the bench and knelt before her. He lifted serious eyes to hers.

"Last night I asked for God's forgiveness. Last night I promised to obey Him all the rest of my days upon this earth. Last night, I finally found freedom."

Tears came to Brianna's eyes and she brushed at them with one hand as they slid warmly down her cheek.

"Today," Garek continued, "I want to give up my freedom. I want to give my oath to you, and I vow it will be the last oath I make. Will you give your oath to me, Brianna? Will you belong to me for all time?"

Leaning forward, Brianna took his face between her palms. She smiled brightly into his eyes before covering his lips with hers. Wrapping her arms around his neck, with her kiss she gave him her answer.

# epilogue

Lady Marie Waverly was wed to Lord Antoine Hormis in Westminster Abbey by King William's good friend, the Bishop Lanfranc.

The magnificent cathedral was a testimony to the love King Edward the Confessor had for the Lord God Almighty.

Although Brianna had been awed by the famous structure, her thoughts were not on the building now. As Marie and Sir Hormis exchanged vows, Brianna's eyes went to the man standing by her side.

Garek took Brianna's hand into his own larger one, and with his eyes, repeated the vows that he and Brianna had exchanged themselves only three months before. Brianna's eyes darkened to sapphire as she in return repeated her vows in her mind. Her heart swelled with love and gratitude that God had allowed her such happiness.

Everything had worked out as God had intended. It had taught Brianna a valuable lesson: Have patience and wait on God's pleasing and perfect will.

Garek lifted her hand to his lips, and regardless of any watchers, slowly kissed each of her fingers. His eyes promised her much more, and Brianna could feel her breathing become uneven as she thought of the days, and nights, to come.

Color bloomed becomingly in her cheeks, and Garek thought her more lovely than the bride standing before the bishop in all her wedding finery.

When the ceremony was over, everyone returned to the king's residence to celebrate. Brianna watched little Matilda beside the king's wife of the same name. Queen Matilda was barely taller than the child beside her.

The woman laughed with the child and when Marie joined the group it became a merry party. Sir Hormis also joined the group, placing a hand possessively on his wife's waist.

Marie smiled up at him, love glowing in her eyes. Little Matilda wedged her way between them, and Brianna was relived to see the smile of welcome the knight bestowed upon her. They would make a fine family.

Garek found his wife watching the small tableau and his eyebrows raised in question.

"I was not sure Sir Hormis would welcome a child when he was so newly married. I am pleased to see that he loves Matilda," Brianna told him.

"He would love her if for no other reason than the fact that he loves Marie."

Brianna nodded. "True, but the child should be loved for herself."

Placing his arm around her waist, Garek gave her a slight hug. "Someday it will be our turn."

Brianna smiled absently. "Would you welcome a son, Garek? Or perhaps a daughter?"

"In time, ma cherie. But for now, let us enjoy our time alone."

Frowning slightly, Brianna told him, "I am afraid our time alone may be limited."

It took a moment for her words to sink in. Surprised, he stared at her. "When?"

"At Christmas time, I think."

A smile spread slowly across his face and his eyes began to glow. "A Christmas child. It is good."

Relieved, Brianna turned to him. "Truly you do not mind?"

"Bien-aimeé, I could not be happier. Je t'aime."

Brianna smiled widely. "I love you, too. When may we go home?"

"I have already told William that we shall be leaving on the morrow. I have a need to feel my own dirt beneath my feet."

Taking her by the hand, Garek made his excuses to the king and his wife and together he and Brianna retired to their own bed chamber.

Later that night, Garek held his wife close and listened to her even breathing. His heart swelled with love and a fierce desire to protect her.

God had truly blessed him with this woman. It amazed him still how the Lord had worked everything out to His own purpose. He was still unsure why God would choose someone so unworthy to be husband to the loving maid he held so close, but he was thankful nonetheless.

In time, harsh memories would be forgotten, and hopefully the land would be united under one leadership with no more need of bloodshed. Garek had no desire to leave his wife for even a short period of time.

Smiling to himself in the darkness, Garek snuggled his wife closer. Let those who had the desire range across the lands and the seas in search of conquest and adventure. As for himself, his wandering days had ended.

# A Letter To Our Readers

Dear Reader:

In order that we might better contribute to your reading enjoyment, we would appreciate your taking a few minutes to respond to the following questions. When completed, please return to the following:

Rebecca Germany, Managing Editor
Heartsong Presents
PO Box 719
Uhrichsville, Ohio 44683

1. Did you enjoy reading *A Light Within?*
   ❑ Very much. I would like to see more books
       by this author!
   ❑ Moderately
       I would have enjoyed it more if _____

   _____

2. Are you a member of **Heartsong Presents**? ❑Yes ❑No
   If no, where did you purchase this book?_____

   _____

3. What influenced your decision to purchase this book? (Check those that apply.)

   ❑ Cover          ❑ Back cover copy

   ❑ Title          ❑ Friends

   ❑ Publicity      ❑ Other_____

4. How would you rate, on a scale from 1 (poor) to 5 (superior), the cover design?_____

5. On a scale from 1 (poor) to 10 (superior), please rate the following elements.

___Heroine     ___Plot

___Hero     ___Inspirational theme

___Setting     ___Secondary characters

6. What settings would you like to see covered in **Heartsong Presents** books?_____

_____

_____

7. What are some inspirational themes you would like to see treated in future books?_____

_____

_____

8. Would you be interested in reading other **Heartsong Presents** titles?    ❏ Yes       ❏ No

9. Please check your age range:
❏ Under 18    ❏ 18-24    ❏ 25-34
❏ 35-45    ❏ 46-55    ❏ Over 55

10. How many hours per week do you read? _____

Name _____

Occupation_____

Address_____

City_____ State_____ Zip_____

Colleen L. Reece takes girls ages 9 to 15 on nail-biting adventures in the Nancy Drew style, but with a clear Christian message. Super sleuth Juli Scott and her savvy friends find love and excitement and learn that it always pays to have a sense of humor. The first two titles in this mystery series are not to be missed.

___*Mysterious Monday*—Julie refuses to believe her father was killed in the line of duty as a policeman. With the help of her new friend Shannon, Julie sets out to reopen the case.

___*Trouble on Tuesday*—Shannon has gotten caught up in fortune telling and an uncanny prediction. In spite of everything her friends try to do, only God can save her from this web of deception.

___*Wednesday Witness*—Being in the wrong place at the wrong time endangers Juli and her friends when they witness a bank robbery.

___*Thursday Trials*—Julie and her friends are called upon to be courtroom witnesses in order to keep the bank robbers from striking again.

# ·········· Presents ··········

## Great Inspirational Romance at a Great Price!

**Heartsong Presents** books are inspirational romances in contemporary and historical settings, designed to give you an enjoyable, spirit-lifting reading experience. You can choose wonderfully written titles from some of today's best authors like Peggy Darty, Sally Laity, Tracie Peterson, Colleen L. Reece, Lauraine Snelling, and many others.

*When ordering quantities less than twelve, above titles are $2.95 each.*
*Not all titles may be available at time of order.*

---

SEND TO: Heartsong Presents Reader's Service
P.O. Box 719, Uhrichsville, Ohio 44683

Please send me the items checked above. I am enclosing $_____.
(please add $1.00 to cover postage per order. OH add 6.25% tax. NJ add 6%). Send check or money order, no cash or C.O.D.s, please.
**To place a credit card order, call 1-800-847-8270.**

NAME _____

ADDRESS _____

CITY/STATE_____ ZIP _____

# Hearts♥ng Presents
## *Love Stories Are Rated G!*

That's for godly, gratifying, and of course, great! If you love a thrilling love story, but don't appreciate the sordidness of some popular paperback romances, **Heartsong Presents** is for you. In fact, **Heartsong Presents** is the *only inspirational romance book club*, the only one featuring love stories where Christian faith is the primary ingredient in a marriage relationship.

Sign up today to receive your first set of four, never before published Christian romances. Send no money now; you will receive a bill with the first shipment. You may cancel at any time without obligation, and if you aren't completely satisfied with any selection, you may return the books for an immediate refund!

Imagine...four new romances every four weeks—two historical, two contemporary—with men and women like you who long to meet the one God has chosen as the love of their lives...all for the low price of $9.97 postpaid.

*To join, simply complete the coupon below and mail to the address provided.* **Heartsong Presents** romances are rated G for another reason: They'll arrive *Godspeed!*